THE
ROSE GATE
a Retelling of Beauty and the Beast

by

HANNA SANDVIG

The 1st Faerie Tale Romance

THE
ROSE GATE

a Retelling of Beauty and the Beast

by

HANNA SANDVIG

For my mother,

Who inspired me to write and dream,
and helped me every step of the way.
This book wouldn't exist without you.

CHAPTER 1

ONCE UPON A TIME, THERE WAS A beautiful princess." I tilted the storybook and showed my preschool class the colorful illustration. "She was also resourceful, creative, and very good at math."

"I don't remember there being math in this story," Avery whispered loudly to little Rory, who sat next to her in the reading circle.

I gave the chubby blond girl a quelling look. "Now, even though the princess was beautiful, smart, and quite healthy, she couldn't resist running around touching pokey things like this spinning wheel. Is it safe, kids, to play with sharp objects?"

"Nooooo," chorused most of the preschool summer reading club.

Rory whispered to Avery, "I like this story better when Miss Chloe reads it."

"So, because the princess was not a careful girl, an evil fairy cursed her to sleep for a hundred years. Her garden got very out of control during this time." I showed the group an illustration of exuberant watercolor roses.

"Now, because of this inconvenient curse..."

"What's an inconvict curse, Miss Isobel?" William's finger was up his nose. Again.

"It's what happens to kids who don't eat enough fruits and vegetables," I warned the class. "And in this case, it kept the princess from doing anything useful for quite a while, and she had to be rescued by a handsome prince who kissed her without permission." I turned the page to show them the picture of the handsome prince kissing Sleeping Beauty. "Kids, don't let anyone kiss you without permission."

"What even is this?" asked a boy from the back row while Avery and Rory sighed dreamily at the image of the prince and princess dancing through fields of roses.

"That was the moral of the story, Charlie." I turned the page. "And the prince and princess got married and lived happily ever after. Once they got to know each other properly and the princess went to university for at least four years to complete a bachelor's."

"Very practical of her." The head librarian leaned against the classroom door, peering at me over her gold-rimmed glasses with amusement.

"Miss Chloe!" Fifteen preschoolers cheered as they ran over and mobbed the older, curly-haired woman.

"Miss Chloe, Miss Isobel didn't tell the story right." Avery put her hands on her hips.

"Ah well, Avery." Miss Chloe gave the girl a hug. "Stories change a little every time they're told. They can't help it."

Miss Chloe passed me a damp rag, and we wiped down the tables as parents arrived to pick up their precious but rather sticky children. "Keep your kitty picture flat, William," I called after the boy, "or all the macaroni will slide off."

"So, what are your plans for the rest of the day, Isobel?" Miss Chloe scraped googly eyes and dry macaroni off the table and into a garbage can.

"I have a new book, and it looks like it'll be a warm afternoon, so I think I'll go for a walk and find a sunny rock to read on. Like a lizard."

"A lizard who reads?"

"Exactly." I tried to peel a gluey piece of construction paper off the table without ripping it. No dice.

"Why doesn't a pretty young thing like you have something more exciting to do?"

I stifled a laugh. People who lived in small towns didn't mean to be ironic when they discussed local excitement. "I'll have you know my book has vampires *and* magic swords in it. It's very exciting."

"You don't want to go to the lake with the other kids?"

"That's more my sister Amber's scene."

Since moving from Vancouver to Pilot Bay halfway through my last semester of high school, I'd done my best to avoid drawing any attention to myself at school, and I had succeeded brilliantly, much to the disgust of my younger sister. I just wasn't interested in wasting my energy trying to break into a social scene where everyone else had been friends since...in utero, probably. Now that school was out, they had all probably forgotten that I existed.

"Don't worry about me and my social life. You and the library kids are enough excitement for a Tuesday." I wiped the last of the glue off the table. Or was that snot? "I'm a happy hermit. Maybe I'll go for a hike—be a healthy, happy hermit."

"There's an old miner's cabin not far from your end of town. Have you hiked up that way?"

"No." I perked up. I hadn't even heard about an old cabin. "Where does the trail start?"

"You know where the ATV track is?" Miss Chloe took my rag and picked up the garbage can. Our battle against grime and glitter was done for today.

I nodded. The track passed behind my back yard, and I'd hiked it a few times. It was nothing special.

"Apparently, if you follow it up the mountain for about a half hour, there's a rock cairn marking the trail to the cabin. It's supposed to be a fairly easy hike."

"You haven't been up there?"

"Oh, I'm not much for the wilderness," Miss Chloe laughed. "Bugs, bears, sinister gingerbread houses—you know how it is."

I nodded politely, but, honestly, after growing up in the city, I couldn't get enough of exploring the woods around Pilot Bay. The Kootenays were still part of British Columbia, but it felt like a different world from Vancouver. I would be sorry to leave the mountains and forests for school in the fall.

"Well, I'll brave the evil witches and check it out. Have a nice day." I gave the head librarian a hug before I grabbed my bag and slipped on my sandals.

"Don't touch any sharp objects," she called after me as I stepped out into the bright sunshine.

Words to live by.

"How was reading club?" asked Lily as I dropped my bag on the kitchen counter. She was flipping through a cookbook. The kitchen was Lily's domain. She'd always been better at mom-type stuff than our mother had.

"Reading club was good. Any day without glitter is a good day." I inspected the cookie jar for treats. "Another day of work, another university credit paid for. Well, maybe half a credit."

Chocolate chip! My sister's chocolate chip cookies were the best. Lily claimed that the secret ingredient was love, but we all knew it was the salted caramel chips she mixed in.

"Glitter is bad?" Lily examined a page in the cookbook.

"Well, glitter isn't inherently bad, but all my clothes are getting shimmery. I found glitter in the pockets of my jeans today on the way to the library. How is that even possible? I haven't worn them all week."

"It's magic." Lily winked. "You know, if you'd enroll in online classes, it would be a lot cheaper. I know you've been accepted into UVIC already, but I'm sure they'd let you put it off for a year or two. You could stay here and save on rent, too."

I shuddered. "Please don't even joke about that. This house was cute when it was our vacation home, but it's lacking some important things. Like insulation. And breathing room."

Six more weeks of sharing a roof with my little sister Amber was plenty. More than plenty.

"It's just something to think about." Lily didn't push it. She never liked to argue. "Should we have taco salad or actual tacos?"

"Actual tacos."

"Actual tacos are more work. Will you be home this afternoon to help make tortillas?"

"You know that they have tortillas at the store, right?"

"A sun-dried-tomato-flavored wheat wrap is not a tortilla. Besides, homemade is always better."

"True enough. I'm just going out for a wander with my book. I won't be too long. Where's Amber?" As if Amber would be any help. Or eat any evil, carb-filled tortillas.

"She's at the beach. Although she keeps complaining that it's not a real beach because there's no ocean."

Amber was probably out drinking on a boat somewhere with her friends from school. For someone so disdainful of small-town life, she sure slipped into it quickly enough.

"Where are you wandering to?" Lily asked. "You and your book?"

I finished my second cookie and grabbed an apple from the fridge to eat as I hiked. "Miss Chloe says there's an old miner's cabin up the mountain behind our place. Up that ATV trail? I'm going to see if I can find it."

"How far is it? I'm not sure I like you being out there by yourself. Sarah from work says there are wolves around here sometimes at night."

"Wolves? Really?" I raised my eyebrows.

"That's the rumor. And cougars. And bears."

"Oh my!" I teased. She gave me a look. "Okay, okay, Mom." My joke fell flat. Gathering up my bag, I gave her a hug. "Thanks for the cookies, Lily."

She kissed the top of my head and I headed upstairs to change.

Lily and I shared a bedroom at the top of the stairs. Amber had claimed the master bedroom on the other half of the small loft for herself. Apparently, she needed the bigger closet. Whatever. Dad had a small room off the kitchen that I suspected was supposed to be a pantry, but I think he was happy to let the upstairs be a feminine domain.

Lily had painted our room a cheery robin's egg blue when we moved in and found bright vintage floral blankets and curtains. My contributions were the strings of white Christmas lights I had brought from my old room and the bookcase bursting with all the books I could fit into my share of the moving boxes. It was cute, which was about as good as it was going to get in here.

I changed into a yellow jersey sundress and pulled on some bike shorts under it. For modesty. You never knew about those wolves and their dirty minds. I grabbed my Kindle off the bed and double-checked the charge before tucking it into my bag. Sunscreen? Check. Ponytail? Check.

As I descended the narrow wooden stairs, the phone rang. And when I say phone, I mean landline. You had to hike into the middle of town and hold your teeth just right to get a lonely bar of connection. Which Amber did twice a day. I had given up and only used my phone as a camera. It wasn't a very good camera.

"Hello, Watson house. No, he's not here." Lily's voice drifted from the living room. "No. I don't know, maybe after six? Hello? Hello?"

"That's a bit rude," she muttered as she hung up the phone.

"It was for Dad?" No one ever called for Dad. Like ever.

"Yeah, but they hung up while I was talking." She gave the phone another glare then handed me a chilly water bottle and a small spray bottle. "Here. If you must go wandering alone in the woods, at least take this."

I gave her a questioning look.

"It's bear spray. Make sure you aim it downwind."

"What if the bear is upwind?" I dropped it into my bag.

"I wonder if I should get you a bell." She tapped her finger on her chin. "Or a large dog."

"I'm leaving now." I pulled my sandals on and headed out the door. "No buying a puppy while I'm gone. Or a tambourine!"

"No, no, a bell for your bag, to let bears know where you are."

"I don't want the bears to know where I am. See you in a couple hours!" I escaped through the bright red front door—Lily's work, of course—and breathed in the smell of pine trees in the sun. A perfect day to be with nobody.

CHAPTER 2

THE SUN BEAT DOWN ON MY SHOULDERS as I hiked along the twin dirt tracks into the forest behind our house. It was gloriously hot out today. The Kootenays got more sun than the coast ever did. My sisters could avoid the heat by staying inside or in the water if they wanted to, but I loved it. I loved the weight of the sun on my skin and the way my dark hair got hot to the touch.

I loved the snap and crackle of grasshoppers springing ahead of me in the long grass.

The wide track that cut behind the back of our cabin was supposedly used by hunters in the fall, but it was abandoned this time of year. We'd get the odd hiker or dog walker, but there were more picturesque hikes to spend your afternoon on, with waterfalls and overlooks to mountain with no epic views, but that suited me just fine. I didn't need epic views. I just needed silence.

Growing up in Vancouver, I'm not sure I even knew what silence was. In the city, there was always this buzz of traffic punctuated by sirens and the occasional crash or bang. Even in our part of the city, where crime was told to kindly keep its dirty feet out, it was never quiet. Add two sisters who liked to chatter and a mother who thought a weekend wasn't a weekend without a dinner party full of very important people, and I usually escaped with my books and my headphones to find a little peace.

When everything fell apart in early March, we moved with Dad to the cabin. One day, when Amber's sniping and Lily's crying and Dad's annoyed muttering about the sniping and the crying got to be too much for me, I ran out the back door with no thought beyond not being in that tiny, loud house. And the forest was waiting for me. It wasn't much to look at in March, a month of mud and potential, but the quiet? The quiet was beautiful.

Now, of course, a forest isn't truly silent. There's always the rustle of leaves, the calls of the birds, and the odd noise in the underbrush you hope is not a large snake. But those noises don't intrude on you. The forest doesn't need anything from you. It just is. And it's content to let you be the same.

At the edge of our yard, the dry grass was eaten up by the bracken fern. The feathery plants were growing tall, above my knees already, and they weren't showing signs of slowing down yet. After wading through the ferns—which had very little regard for where the trail edges were—I reached the aspens with their slim, white trunks and bright green leaves that shimmered and whispered in the slightest breeze. I pulled my sandals off and tucked them in my bag so I could enjoy the earth beneath my feet as I walked. There hadn't been much for dirt paths in the city, and wearing shoes felt like taking this one for granted.

The birds weren't making much noise as I walked along in the afternoon heat, but I caught a flash of a red head as a little woodpecker zipped across the trail ahead of me. I could hear a chatter overhead and I glanced up, wary of the squirrels who had thrown nuts down at me on previous hikes. The aspens gave way to towering, sweet-smelling ponderosa pine, and I fell into a rhythm as I walked.

The double tracks slanted uphill, and I kept my eyes open for the cairn Miss Chloe had mentioned. Even with close attention, I almost missed it because the top two rocks had fallen off into the grass. I picked one up, warm from the sun on one side, cool from the earth on the other, and balanced it on the knee-high tower of rocks. I grabbed the second rock and turned it over. Interesting. The outline of a symbol was carved into the smooth stone. I traced my finger over the worn lines, three inter-locking spirals, and set it on the top of the cairn before hunting for the path it marked.

I would never have seen the trail without the marker. It was little more than a deer path cutting deeper into the forest. The shrubs bent into the trail, leaving little white scratches on my legs as I walked. The forest darkened as the trees grew taller. Within a few steps, I had almost lost the trail, but I could see the brightening of a clearing up ahead. It must be the cabin.

The forest lightened as I walked through another pale, graceful aspen grove into the clearing. I caught a flash of red as I stepped past the last trees. Turning back, I saw dark red roses in the trees. They had grown up over the path, making a natural arch across the branches of two trees before trailing down the trunk on the other side. The heat warmed my shoulders in the clearing as I examined the velvety blossoms, petals spread open to face the sun. The roses were unexpected and beautiful but not what I was here to find.

I turned back to the clearing. It was quieter than the forest. No grasshoppers snapped in front of me as I walked through the meadow. I ran my hands over a few black-eyed Susans poking their yellow faces above the tall grass.

I stopped to examine the cabin before going in. It was built of interlocking logs, and the low-peaked roof was covered in moss and sprouting small plants. Aspen saplings crowded it on one side, and a single determined tree appeared to have sprouted through the middle of the roof as the forest reclaimed the old structure.

None of this made it look particularly safe, but it had stood this long. Surely it wouldn't cave in on me if I went inside? I eyed the rough floorboards and slipped my sandals back on to protect me from splinters and spiders. Hopefully not spiders.

I stepped through the doorway, and...I guess I was inside now? I don't know what I had expected but as I turned around, the space was lit only by light from the doorway and from a square of sunlight coming through the little side window. I felt a bit let down. Shouldn't there be ghosts? Mysterious documents? Photos of a lost love? Instead, I found nothing but a couple of beer bottles in the corner suggesting I wasn't the only person to hike up here. That was it.

I took one more look around the cabin. *Terry wuz here!* proclaimed the carved words over the door. Thanks, Terry. I shrugged and went back out into the sun.

I explored the meadow around the cabin. It was very meadowy. That done, I decided to head back down the mountain and found myself back in front of the roses. The local wild roses had finished blooming a couple weeks ago, but these deep red blossoms were plentiful as they climbed up the tree and spread across its branches to reach for the tree on the other side of me. I followed their path around and down the second tree and touched a tightly closed bloom with my fingertip.

It vibrated softly under my touch, sending a humming sensation up my arm. I jerked my hand back and eyed the rose suspiciously. It remained closed, as if ignoring me.

Wait, hadn't the roses been open when I walked past them earlier? I examined the roses on the other tree, and, sure enough, all the roses were curled shut. Huh. Did roses do that? I honestly hadn't ever given their habits much thought. I watched them for a minute to see if they had any other tricks to pull, but they just sat there. Closed. I touched another one to see if it would give me the same strange humming feeling, but I couldn't tell for sure.

I shook my head and checked the time on my phone. Time to head home if I wanted to help Lily make dinner. I drank some water, tucked my sandals back into my bag, and after another glance at the strange roses, I headed into the forest again, following the faint path.

As I entered the forest, I thought I caught a glimpse of something large and dark from the corner of my eye, and my hand fumbled for Lily's bear spray while I scanned through the trees. Nothing. I shook my head and started down the path toward home.

My imagination was clearly on overdrive today. Maybe I should switch to reading nonfiction for a few days.

CHAPTER 3

"D ID YOU MAKE IT OUT TO THE cabin?" asked Miss Chloe as we set up the day's craft on Monday morning. Egg carton mushrooms with not only glitter but also some sort of rainbow sand. Heaven help us.

"I did." I carefully filled a little bowl with red sand. "Did you know there are roses out there? Like, garden roses? Do you know why?"

"I've heard that, but I don't know the story behind them. Interesting that they've survived all this time without anyone taking care of them."

"It's odd, right? Also, I could swear they were open when I got there, but they looked closed when I left." I didn't mention the humming feeling. I sounded crazy

"Maybe it was getting late? There are some rose varieties that close at night." Miss Chloe squinted as she filled little paper cups with craft glue.

"It wasn't that late, only three o'clock maybe? I must have imagined it." I hadn't imagined it.

"I've always loved roses, but I'm not an expert. However, the Pilot Bay Garden Club meets here at the library every week. If you took a photo of the roses, I could show it to them. Maybe they could identify the variety?"

"Oh, that could be interesting. I'll try and hike back up there this week and take a picture for you." I wanted to check on the roses again with my own eyes anyway, to be sure my memory wasn't playing tricks on me.

Kids trickled into the room as parents dropped them off and made a break for freedom. I pushed the narcoleptic roses to the back of my mind and turned my attention to sweet, if sometimes sticky, hugs from my favorite preschoolers.

I didn't get back to the miner's cabin as soon as I wanted to. The weekend came, and without the excuse of my work at the library, my sisters coerced me into beach time on Saturday. It was fine. I had a book. But my mind wasn't interested in vampire hunters and insisted on drifting back to the woods and the scent of roses.

"Like wild roses?" asked Lily when I tried to explain the strange flowers as we sat on our towels. Our legs were covered with sand, and we were waiting for the sun to bake it sufficiently to be brushed off before we put our sandals on.

"No, red roses, like the pink ones that grew in the back garden at home. Except, you know, red." And deep and velvety and...watchful.

"Isn't that strange? Garden roses in the woods? Amber, do you think that's strange?" Lily poked our little sister, who was giving her best impression of a very tanned coma patient on the towel next to us.

"Very strange," Amber mumbled without opening her eyes.

"Hmm, I never really thought of that. I guess a gnarly old gold miner wouldn't be likely to plant roses out in the woods. Maybe he had a sweetheart to make happy?" I paused to imagine a star-crossed gold miner and his rose-loving lady.

"Maybe a bear ate some rose hips in town and pooped them out by the cabin," suggested Amber, who was clearly paying more attention than she wanted to.

"A born romantic here," laughed Lily, pouring a little water from her water bottle onto Amber's bronzed stomach. The shriek that followed was well worth the half hour of grumbling as we trekked back from the lake to our cabin.

The next day I guilted everyone into going to our little town church with me. No one else in my family had ever been much for religion, but Lily knew it was important to me. Amber only tagged along because, inexplicably, it was one of the three spots in town with any cell signal. Divine service intervention. I liked to think some of the pastor's message sank in, even if she spent the majority of the time texting.

That afternoon it rained, and it kept raining until the next day.

I dodged puddles through the drizzle as I walked home from the library. I loved that I could walk anywhere I needed to go in Pilot Bay. From my house, it was ten minutes to the library, fifteen to church or the bookstore, seventeen to the bakery, and thirty to the beach. No buses needed and no fighting through traffic. How long had it taken me to get to the miner's cabin? Forty-five minutes, maybe? Was it worth trying to wander out there after dinner so I could get that photo for the garden club to look at?

Lightning flashed in the distance over the lake, followed closely by a rumble that echoed between the mountains. I sighed. Not today. Maybe I could convince Lily to make cookies while the weather was cool enough to run the oven. I should have brought an umbrella. I was soaked by the time I pushed through our bright red front door. I ducked into the bathroom to grab a towel for my hair.

"It's ridiculous!" Amber griped from the kitchen. "I just want to buy shoes. But there are no shoe stores. Not for miles! The lady at the bakery told me to check at the hardware store. Do you know what they sell at the hardware store?"

"Hmm?" Lily was clearly only listening with half her attention. Amber tended to get grumbly when the weather forced her to spend too much time in close quarters with the rest of us.

"Crocs! They sell Crocs. And also, little decorations you can put in the holes of the Crocs to make them pretty. With like, Dora or Elmo on them."

Lily laughed.

"It's not funny. How do people live here? And why? And when can we leeeeave and go back to civilization?"

I peeked into the doorway. Sure enough, Amber sat at the kitchen table drinking a beer and poking at her phone.

"Nice hat," Amber said as I came in. "So, what did we do today? Hug trees? Teach orphans to read? Hold a prayer vigil for the Middle East?"

An absolute joy. I ignored her as I finished drying off my hair and draped my towel over the back of a chair. "Whatcha making?" I peered over Lily's arm.

"Snickerdoodles." Lily tapped the recipe. Of course, Amber's favorite. Lily was too nice for her own good. Amber would never say thank you. She would grump about

33

Lily trying to make her fat and then eat half the batch at night when no one could see her do it.

"So, Bel, how would you like to lend me twenty dollars?" askedAmber sweetly. "It's like giving to charity, only more fun."

"Tempting, but no." I already regretted coming into the kitchen. Was it bad of me to want to leave her to Lily? I stole a pinch of creamed sugar and butter, the most satisfying stage of cookie dough, and Lily smacked my knuckles lightly with her wooden spoon.

"Run! Save yourself," she said under her breath.

"I'll pay you back." Amber flipped her dark hair over her shoulder. "I need to bring a six-pack to the party tonight. It's embarrassing freeloading all the time!"

"How is taking my money not freeloading?" I asked. "Anyway, it's all in my savings account for school. Besides…"

"I'm legally underage, blah, blah, freaking blah." The eye-rolls were real as she took another swig of her beer.

I took Lily's advice and turned to leave, snagging my towel.

"You're also terrible at asking for favors," I shot back from the doorway.

"You could make some money by babysitting?" suggested Lily.

Amber and I turned to her in horror. Honestly, the idea of Amber in charge of small children was terrifying.

"Or not?" Lily grimaced and added flour to the bowl.

Amber refocused on begging Lily for money, and I escaped up the stairs as Lily explained that we needed her money for things like food. I shut the door and pretended I couldn't hear them anymore as I flopped onto the bed. The rain tapped on the cabin's tin roof, each drip reminding me that I was trapped inside, the silence of the forest out of reach. Finally, I gave up and grabbed headphones and my book, escaping the walls that were closing me in and the muffled arguing below in the only way I could.

It was even worse when Dad got home from his job at the gas station. Most days, Amber simply didn't acknowledge his existence, but she was out for blood tonight. By suppertime, both of them were drinking, which never improved things.

"Know what I miss?" Amber stabbed a square of chicken breast violently and swirled it around in her pasta sauce.

"Your manners?" asked Lily sweetly. Clearly, Amber was getting under even her thick skin by now.

"No." Amber chewed her chicken while appearing to seriously consider the question. "I can't say that I do. Live music, though. I miss that."

I ate my pasta and peeked past her head out the window. Was it still raining? Maybe less? Maybe I could go for a hike after supper.

"Did you know," continued Amber conversationally, "that Sonic Mob is playing in Nelson? They are, as I'm sure you all remember, my favorite band. And that's only two hours from here."

We all kept eating, waiting for her to get to her point. It shouldn't take long.

"But!" Amber's voice went up a notch. She was getting into the swing of it now. "Even if I could get the money for a ticket, which no one will give me, I couldn't drive there because...? Anyone?"

No one answered her.

"I have no car!"

And she had now achieved full ranting mode.

"Lily has no car. Bel has no car. And, of course, Dad has no car. Because he stupidly lost it all and moved us out to this hole of a town with no way to even get out!"

I winced, my appetite quickly disappearing.

"Amber Watson!" protested Lily.

"What, Lily? It's true! Don't you 'Amber' me." Amber waved her fork threateningly in Lily's direction. "Stop acting like such a saint, Lily! You make out like it's no big deal. Like you decided to come home and help out, when we all know you didn't have the money to stay in school after your semester finished. Because Dad cleared out our college funds."

Dad slammed down his beer bottle, making all of us jump. "You have no idea what I have done for you. For this family."

"You made Mom leave!" Amber's voice rose higher, tears in her eyes now. "She left because of you, and you aren't even trying to get her back."

That was enough. The pressure started to build behind my eyes, but I *would not* cry at the dinner table. I didn't even know who I was more upset with. Lily, for pretending everything was okay when Amber was right. It wasn't okay. Amber, for not even trying to be a part of this family anymore. Dad, for...I didn't even know what had happened to our money exactly, but like Amber said, everything had disappeared, from our cars and our house to our future.

Or was I upset with Mom? But I couldn't face thinking about her right now. I shoved my chair back as they kept arguing and dashed for the front door, stopping to sling my bag over my shoulder. I shuffled into my flip-flops before I flung the door open. The rain had stopped, and for a moment, I just stood there with the fresh air on my flushed cheeks. I stepped through the doorway, but Lily caught it as I swung it closed behind me.

"Are you okay?" She looked desperate.

"None of us are okay, Lily." I felt too tired to explain. "I just need some peace and some fresh air."

"It's too late. You could run into something."

"Bears, wolves, rabid squirrels. I know."

"Isobel..." she started testily.

"I won't go far," I lied. "I'll keep an eye on the time," I added more truthfully. But I still had a couple of hours before dark.

"Be reasonable, Isobel." Lily used her most annoying parental tone and put her hand on my wrist.

Silently, I twisted out of her grasp and headed for the forest.

Before I reached the path, I glanced back. Lily sat on the steps by the door with her eyes closed as Amber and Dad yelled at each other inside. Six more weeks of summer.

CHAPTER 4

I CRASHED THROUGH THE FOREST, NOT EVEN seeing the trees as a rogue tear or two made their way down my cheeks. Amber was getting angrier lately, and I didn't know how to be around her. It wasn't until I approached the meadow that my breathing grew steadier and I began to register my surroundings. My stomach sank. I'd badly misjudged the amount of remaining daylight. The days were already growing shorter, and while it wasn't twilight yet, the sun had dipped behind the mountain already.

The drizzle started up again, and the dark clouds made the forest even darker. I slipped on a muddy patch of trail and landed on my butt. I stayed there, leaning back against a tree, rethinking my recent life choices. On the downside, I could get eaten by wolves in the dark or slip on the way back down the mountain and break my neck. On the plus side, that still sounded like an improvement over listening to Amber and Dad argue. I pulled myself back up to my feet. I was almost at the miner's cabin anyway. I might as well go look at the stupid roses again before I went home...or died trying.

The cabin seemed dismal in the rain, the open door a black hole in the twilight. I stepped into the clearing through the damp grass, soaking my legs and the hem of my dress as I went. I turned to see what the roses were up to. Each deep red blossom was pulled shut, which seemed sensible. I tapped one with my finger and drew back in surprise as it shifted slightly. I watched the rose skeptically, but it didn't move. At least, I didn't think so? I took a mental picture of it, then closed my eyes tightly and counted to ten. I opened them and looked at the rose. I was sure a couple of petals were slowly unfurling. I closed my eyes again and counted to a hundred.

"Aha!" I accused the rose. "You're opening."

The rose ignored me and continued moving so slowly I could never be sure I was actually seeing anything at all, but when I looked at the arch as a whole, the roses were definitely opening. Opening just in time for...night? Not only did that make no sense at all, but the roses had been closing the previous afternoon. They clearly had a complete disregard for the laws of nature and their surroundings. I pulled out my phone and took a really grainy photo of the most open blossom I could find. I could show it to the garden club and see if they could give me some answers. A photo wouldn't prove how oddly the roses were acting though. Should I take a video?

I jumped as a crash of thunder overhead brought my attention back to my surroundings. Time to head home before the drizzle became a storm.

The path felt even muckier on the way back down, and my feet slid around so much in my flip-flops that I lost a sandal in the mud. As I bent down to pick it up, I heard a soft sound behind me, and all the hair rose on the back of my neck. Surely it was just my imagination.

Then I heard a twig snap. I slowly straightened up, my heart pounding, and turned to see the pale shape of a large gray wolf a couple of paces behind me on the path.

Well, crap.

I gulped, and everything I'd ever heard about wolves crashed through my head.

They're more afraid of you than you are of them.

The wolf took a step toward me. It didn't strike me as afraid.

Don't stare them down. They'll take it as a threat.

Another wolf stepped out from behind a tree, and I found myself staring into its bright eyes. Crap, crap, crap.

And most importantly…

A third wolf growled on my left, much too close.

A wolf pack hunts on the chase, so stay calm…

I took a step back, and the first wolf took a step forward.

And whatever you do, do not run.

The wolf tipped its head back and howled. All rational thought left me as I heard the howl echoed around me by considerably more wolves than the three I could see. I couldn't help it.

I ran.

I slid and scraped down the muddy slope, my sandals lost behind me, and my bag snagging on branches as I went. With every step, I expected to feel jaws closing on my heels, but the attack never came. I dared a glance back, nearly tripping over a tree root. The wolves ran close behind me. They didn't need to catch up to me. They were waiting for me to get tired or fall. And it was only a matter of time.

My breaths came in sharp and quick as I dodged branches, and my bare feet bled from rocks I didn't have time to avoid. I could see the forest getting lighter ahead as I approached the wider ATV road, but that wasn't much help. I was still a half hour's walk from the house. The wolves yipped at each other all around me. The path grew harder to see as the forest darkened. Then, my toe hit a rock. Pain coursed through my foot. As I tried to regain my balance, my other ankle rolled, and I went down.

A wolf was on me before I even hit the ground, my arms flung up to protect my face, and I screamed as teeth sank into my left forearm. But in that breath between life and death, my ears rang with a deep breathy roar.

The wolf yelped and scrambled back as a giant shape slammed down beside me. My heart pounded faster. This wasn't salvation, for if there was anything more terrifying than wolves, it was a grizzly bear, and by the hump on its back this one was a male and huge. It had a scarred muzzle and missing left eye that gave it the look of a fighter.

The bear let out a breathy snuff of warning. The lead wolf tried to break around him to get to me again. With another terrifying roar, the bear captured the full attention of the wolves. The pack growled as they shifted their positions to take on this larger challenge.

I wasn't about to wait around and see who won. I scrambled to my feet and turned to run, but my twisted ankle betrayed me. I fell again, tumbling down the slippery bank and slamming my head into a rock.

When I woke up, my first happy thought was that I was clearly not dead. I was very much alive, but my happiness was short-lived because I was also being dragged through the forest by my arm. By the bear. The remaining daylight had faded, and while I couldn't see anything, I could feel the hot breath of the bear as he huffed and snorted in the dark. His teeth were painfully tight on my arm but weren't through my skin. My breath came in panicky gasps. We had watched a bear safety video in school last spring. If you had the poor luck to run across an aggressive grizzly, your best chance for survival was playing dead. I tried to stay limp, but then I remembered the survivor in the video. She had, after being mauled and partly scalped, been buried alive for the bear to eat later. She later dug herself out and made it to safety.

The idea of being eaten was bad enough, but being buried alive was one step too far. I panicked, scrambling my feet on the ground and attempting to twist away, which did nothing but scrape my arm painfully against teeth before the bear blessedly let go. I could see dimly now. The moon must have come out from behind the clouds because it was suddenly bright enough to make out some things. I could see my feet, but no further than that. I pushed myself up in an attempt to run, but I'd forgotten about my injured ankle, and it gave way once again.

Strong arms caught me, and I fought against them as well, confused but in no mood to stay and see what had happened to the bear.

"Shh, *Àlainn*," came a soft voice by my ear. "Sleep."

And those arms caught me up against a solid body that began walking as a sudden, overwhelming wave of drowsiness overcame me. I did, indeed, sleep, the scent of roses surrounding me.

THE ROSE GATE

PART 2

CHAPTER 5

"THERE YOU GO, ÀLAINN," SAID A LOW, gentle voice.
I opened my eyes. A big beast of a man hovered
over me. He had a brown, bushy beard, and his
long hair had twigs stuck in it. It was his face, however,
that was truly shocking. One gray eye stared into mine, but
the other side of his face was sliced with old scars from
top to bottom, his left eye completely gone. What had
happened to him?

I lay on some sort of velvet couch as he tied a bandage
around my injured arm. The strip of cloth looked much
cleaner than I would have expected, given the ragged state
of his dark clothes.

I shrank back from his touch and glanced wildly
around me. Stone walls and gilded furniture were lit by
sunshine pouring through the velvet-draped window. This

was not the miner's cabin. And how long had I been unconscious? Why did my arm not hurt more? The wolf bite should have been throbbing, but it was just a dull ache.

The man reached toward my bandaged arm, and I jumped, pulling back from the one-eyed monster.

He made a shushing noise, like you would to a crying baby or a skittish animal, but I was not shushed. I needed to get out of there.

"You see, my lord," said a raccoon, popping its head up beside the bed. "I told you to shave. You look terrifying."

I blinked at the raccoon. Nope, this was not okay.

"What sort of drugs did you give me?!" I shrieked at the beastly man, who drew back, looking startled. I kicked off the light blanket covering my legs and tumbled to the floor.

"No, I didn't give you anything. You don't understand!" The man reached for me, but I scrambled away from him and got to my feet.

"Where did you bring me?" My voice rose as I edged toward the door.

He started toward me, and I didn't wait for an answer. I bolted for the door and swung myself out into the hallway. Whatever this place was, it was huge, but the massive stairway to my left seemed promising, so I ran to it, my bare feet sinking into the thick rug that ran down the middle of the stone floor. I spun down the twisting stairwell.

I had no time to waste. The one-eyed man looked about a foot and a half taller than me. He'd catch up to me quickly.

But I had terror on my side, and stone stairs were much easier to navigate than a slippery path in the dark. My twisted ankle seemed completely healed, and even the bite on my arm was more itchy than painful. How long had I been asleep?

I stumbled into a foyer and got a brief impression of gilded mirrors and glass lanterns before I pulled open the heavy oak doors. I paused and sneezed in the bright sunshine.

"Wait!" The man sounded close behind me.

Too close.

Nope, not waiting. I yelped as my feet hit the gravel path at the bottom of the stairs. I ignored the sharp little rocks as I passed exuberant rose bushes edging the path. A high stone wall surrounded the garden, but at the end of the path, a stone arch covered in roses formed a perfectly circular gate. I could vaguely make out a dirt trail on the other side. It must be the way out.

"It's not safe!"

I glanced back and almost tripped at the sight of the grand stone castle behind me. How far from home was I? Surely, I would have heard if there was a castle anywhere near Pilot Bay?

A question for another time. I needed to focus on escaping the crazed man behind me.

He had almost caught up to me now. "You need to wait until the sun comes up."

"It's daytime. What are you even talking about!?" I didn't wait for an answer as I dashed through the rose gate toward freedom.

And plunged into darkness.

My feet slid on the muddy path, and my eyes strained to adjust to the sudden lack of sunlight. My shoulder smacked against a tree, and I held onto it to keep myself from falling.

I was back in the forest where the wolves had been chasing me. I heard a soft snarl. The wolves were still chasing me.

It was as if the castle with the roses and the talking raccoon had been a vivid dream.

Which, given the talking raccoon, actually made a lot of sense.

My eyes adjusted to the dark just in time to see a wolf launch itself at me. Then a breathy snarl made me flinch to the side as the giant grizzly bear appeared behind me. The bear knocked the first wolf to the ground, but three more leapt onto him, teeth sinking into his shoulder and foreleg. I stumbled back a couple of steps and found myself blinking in the bright rose garden again.

What?

It had to be some sort of…portal? Magic doorway? I was back at the castle, and the forest with the wolves was somehow on the other side. And so was that bear who had now saved my life twice. He'd been covered in wolves when I left. He was pretty big, but those odds didn't seem fair.

I spied an old pitchfork leaning against the garden wall. This was a terrible idea. I grabbed it anyway and jumped back through the arch of roses.

Darkness swallowed me again, but I swung the pitchfork with all my might at the wolf on the grizzly's shoulder, yelling at the top of my lungs. After all, she who hesitates is lost, right?

The wolf fell to the ground, dazed, and the bear and wolves all paused and stared at me in shock. Well, yes, I was surprised too, but I rammed into the bear with my shoulder in an attempt to push him back through the portal. Of course, nothing happened as he was roughly four times my size. The wolves began to circle back around to us, snarling.

"Move!" I yelled. He blinked at me, then turned and tumbled backward, disappearing into thin air. I ran after him, praying that whatever magic was at work here, the wolves would be unable to follow us.

The smell of roses washed over me again, and I stood back in the garden, the stone castle basking in the afternoon sun.

The bear was nowhere to be seen. Instead the tall, dark, and scraggly mountain man stood in front of me, swaying on his feet. Blood dripped from his arm and soaked through the shoulder of his dark shirt. I supposed in a world with magic portals and talking forest creatures I shouldn't have been surprised, but…

"You're the bear."

He nodded, and what I could see of his face between the hair and the beard seemed pale under the scars.

"And when you told me to wait until sunrise, you didn't mean that sun, did you?" I pointed up at the cheery midday sun.

"I did not."

"Okay, two more questions for you." I took a deep breath. This was clearly crazy. "Where am I? And are you going to pass out on me?"

"This is Kilinaire Castle," he replied. "You're in Tír na nÓg."

"Tirna-what-now?"

"Faerie," he said. "You're in Faerie. As for your second question, I hope not. But can we please go back inside now? I believe all the medical supplies are still laid out in the parlor." He touched his injured shoulder gingerly.

"All right, Bear." I motioned for him to lead the way. "Back to the castle we go. But no fainting on me. You'd squash me like a bug."

CHAPTER 6

THE CASTLE LOOKED EVEN MORE IMPRESSIVE NOW that I wasn't fleeing for my life. It didn't seem terribly big as far as castles went. More like Downton Abbey size than Windsor Castle size. But it was beautiful, all built of light gray stone with small graceful towers on the corners and a taller tower rising up from behind, all capped in roofs of bluey green.

Up a riser of stone steps, columns flanked the entrance. The raccoon was anxiously waiting for us by the carved oak doors, still open from my abrupt departure.

"Ena." The mountain man looked down at the raccoon. "Send Tait to my chamber with the bandages and come help me with my shoulder once you've made our guest comfortable." He turned his unsettling one-eyed gaze on me. "What was your name?"

"Is this a trick?" I narrowed my eyes.

"What do you mean?"

"If I tell you my name, are you going to use it in some sort of magic spell? Or control me? Isn't that what happens in faerie stories?"

"I was going to use it to talk to you in a friendlier manner, but that's clearly wishful thinking." He ran his hand through his messy hair, giving me an exasperated look.

"Well then, what's your name?"

"You're not going to tell me, are you?"

"First, tell me what it was you called me earlier. Ayleen? Were you trying to guess my name to keep me here? Because that's not it." I was probably being ridiculous, but I didn't care. I didn't have any idea what was going on, and it made me grumpy.

He glared at me with his one eye, blood dripping down his arm and then turned wordlessly and hauled himself back up those winding stairs. I heard him grumbling something about ungrateful women and hot baths. Should I be concerned about his shoulder? I did feel bad about the wolves.

"He'll be fine," said a voice by my knee. Ah yes, the raccoon. Ena? Was this the same raccoon as earlier, or was the castle overrun with talking raccoons? "Are you going to scream again?" Its voice sounded like a middle-aged woman with a brisk Irish accent.

"I don't think so?"

"Good. One bout of hysteria is quite enough for today. Now, it appears you will be our guest for the time being. I'm Ena, the housekeeper. Would you like a bath first or lunch?"

"Um, lunch? Are you sure he's okay?" I felt slightly responsible for his injuries. Although he really could have explained things better when I woke up.

"The prince is being taken care of. Now, let's take care of you. Come along." She dropped down onto all fours and padded off down the hallway.

"He's a prince?" I followed her down a flight of stone stairs, ducking my head to avoid hitting the low ceiling above the steps. My expectations of a faerie prince clearly did not line up with reality.

"Yes, yes. Prince of the Rose Court, Kilinaire Castle, and the surrounding area. Mind your head now. The kitchen isn't built for height. The *Tuatha Dé Danann* don't spend a lot of time downstairs."

"Who?" I ducked under the low stone archway into the kitchen.

"Tuatha Dé Danann. High Fae. Lords and ladies. Tall folk. Take a seat."

I obediently sat on a short wooden bench, my legs folding awkwardly under me. The kitchen was cozy, with a vaulted ceiling that gave me just enough room to not crack my head on it, although the copper pots hanging above could still be dangerous. I sat at a low table in the middle of the room, where a couple of beavers and a fox worked busily. Another beaver stirred something in a large pot hanging over a fire, and I also noticed a stack of bricks in the corner. Probably an oven? It could have been overly warm, but a small door opposite the stairwell was propped open to let in a light breeze.

"Deirdre." The raccoon turned to the little fox. "Go and draw a bath in the blue room, if you please."

"Yes, ma'am," yipped the fox. She scurried out of the room.

A beaver slid a bowl of stew with a spoon in it over to me. Chunks of vegetables and meat floated in a rich-looking broth. It smelled amazing. I took a bite. It tasted amazing. I eyed a piece of vegetable that appeared to have been torn, gnawed, or clawed into size and decided not to ask too many questions about the food preparation here.

"Now, my dear." The furry housekeeper popped up onto the bench beside me. "You'll need to bathe and change, and then you might want a nap before dinner. It can be a bit of an adjustment changing times between Faerie and the human world."

"If I'm in Faerie…" I considered my most pressing question as I swallowed a bite of stew. "Then…why aren't you faeries?" Was that rude?

"Oh, we are, of course. It's the curse. It's rather a long story. I'll let the prince explain it all at dinner." The raccoon bustled off, and I heard her talking to one of the beavers about dinner plans.

I finished my stew, trying not to stare at the beaver to my left who was deftly cracking eggs with one paw and whisking them into a bowl with the other.

"All done then?"

I nodded, and the raccoon took my bowl away. Then she led me out of the kitchen, chattering about how lovely it was to have a guest and how long it had been. I tried to keep track of the twists and turns, but I was hopelessly lost by the time she pushed open yet another carved oak door.

It was like something out of a storybook. My bare feet sank into the dark blue plush rug that covered most of the cool stone floor. A huge fireplace—unlit on this sunny day—dominated one corner, flanked by a blue-velvet, stuffed chair and a chaise lounge, making a cozy spot for reading or conversation—but, let's be real, reading. I trailed my fingers along a polished wood end table on my way to the windows on the opposite wall. Bright afternoon light shone through diamond-shaped panes of glass. Sinking onto the velvet-padded window seat, I looked out at pink roses climbing around the window. Sections of the glass were turned open to let the scent of blossoms drift in. I poked my head out and saw the rose garden I had run through earlier down below, the green hedges making a maze around gravel paths. Turning back to the room, I admired the huge four-poster bed of warm carved wood. Gauzy curtains hung from its canopy and stirred gently in the breeze from the windows. It was covered with so many soft blue pillows and throws, it looked like you might risk drowning to sleep in it.

"This will be your room while you stay with us." Ena gestured to the wall opposite the bed. "The toilet, bathing room, and closet are here, here, and here." She pointed to each doorway in turn. "You'll want to have a bath and then a rest before dinner, I presume, as it's currently night in your world."

My head was spinning, but a bath did sound good. I stood up quickly and was relieved to see the mud and twigs covering me hadn't made a mess of the upholstery.

"So, you're actually a faerie? Like with wings?" I was still having trouble with the talking raccoon part. I'm not sure why meeting a faerie seemed more plausible.

"Faerie, yes. Wings, no. I'm a brownie, my dear, not a piskie after all."

"Right. Okay. Bath through there?" I pointed at the middle door.

"That's right. Deirdre should have gotten it ready for you. I'll find you a nightgown and be on my way. I'll send for you at dinnertime."

"Okay." I started into the room, skirting around the largest rug to reach the bathroom. "Um, thank you, Ena."

"We are truly happy to have you here. Now, enjoy your bath."

I did. The bathroom was huge, which I should have guessed after seeing the bedroom. Frosted windows let the light stream in, and a gold and crystal chandelier hung from the high wooden beams overhead. Everything else was a polished white stone. Steps led up to a vast sunken tub that I was relieved to see had taps.

I'd been afraid the castle wouldn't have plumbing and poor Deirdre the fox would have carried buckets of water from a pump outside or something. Or she might have used foxy magic, I supposed. I wasn't clear on the rules. Anyway, I shucked off my clothes and eased into the steaming tub with no guilt about fox mistreatment.

I hadn't thought I was that tired, but as the hot water relaxed my tense muscles, my eyes grew heavy. The evening of running and fighting, and yes, some screaming, had taken a toll on me. Taking a bath for as long as I wanted was a luxury I hadn't enjoyed since we moved to Pilot Bay, at least not without my sisters wandering in and out of our one bathroom ten times an hour, and I stayed in until the water cooled.

I stepped out of the tub and wrapped a large, fluffy blue towel around myself and padded over to the doorway. Peeking out into the room, I checked to make sure it was empty and the door to the hallway was closed. A sleeveless white nightgown was draped across the foot of the bed. I slipped it over my head, and the soft fabric drifted down to my ankles. After clambering up onto the bed and shoving ninety percent of the pillows to the other side, I quickly fell asleep.

CHAPTER 7

I WOKE UP TO AFTERNOON LIGHT AND a knocking at my door. Where was I? It was clearly not morning and not my quilt-covered bottom bunk in the cabin. Apparently, the castle full of talking animals and grumpy bear men had not been a dream. I yawned groggily. I'm not much of a napper, and my body was convinced it was the middle of the night. Faerieland jet lag? Ugh, my mouth tasted funny.

The knocking persisted.

"Hello?" I managed to say through a yawn.

I heard the rattle of a doorknob, and the bottom half of my bedroom door swung open to reveal Ena. The raccoon was sitting neatly on her haunches beside the little fox from the kitchen.

"Good afternoon." Ena rested a paw on the fox's shoulder. "This is Deirdre. She'll attend to your needs while you're our guest. She's a bit shy. She's never met a human. But she's absolutely magic with clothes and hair."

"Pleased to meet you, my lady." The foxy lady's maid bobbed her head in greeting.

"Oh, um, thank you. It's nice to meet you, Deirdre." I paused. "I didn't know the door split in half like that."

"We aren't all tall enough to reach the same door-knobs, now are we?" tutted Ena. "May we come in?"

"Oh, of course!" I slid out of the huge bed.

The furry ladies scurried over to the first door, the one I hadn't been through yet, and with a light nudge, Deirdre pushed the bottom half of the door open. Apparently, they were all built that way. I opened the top half and followed them into a small, dark room smelling of cedar and fabric. Ena chittered something I didn't understand—maybe it was Irish?—and the room lit up as a crystal chandelier brightened overhead.

"How did you do that?" I gaped at the lamp.

"Just a small magic, my dear."

Ena and the fox spoke back and forth in that language I didn't understand. Deirdre seemed hesitant, but Ena was firm in her request.

"Alright, then." The fox eyed me critically before turning to a wall of dresses and flipping through them with her paws. The room was like a big walk-in closet, with clothes hanging on two walls, and chests and racks of shoes and boots on the third. One corner was dominated by a tall, ornate mirror, and I caught sight of myself looking like a medieval ghost in my white nightgown. I probably shouldn't have slept on my wet hair.

The fox waved me over with a fluid string of words, one paw on a light blue dress. She tugged the skirt, and I obediently took the dress off its hanger. Then she and Ena bustled off to a trunk while I changed. The dress was light and silky with little capped sleeves and gold trim along the square neckline. It laced up the front, and a full skirt pooled around my feet on the floor. The laces allowed the top to adjust to my figure, but...

"I can't go out like this," I informed the furry faeries, gesturing to the four inches of cleavage.

"Hmm, yes, I see what you mean. You have rather more up top than she did." Ena eyed me thoughtfully.

"Than who?"

But she ignored me and consulted with Deirdre, who pulled a silvery gray silk scarf from a trunk and gestured for me to kneel down to her level. She expertly folded and tucked the scarf around the back of my neck and then crossed it and tucked it into the front of the dress, giving me more coverage. I peeked in the mirror. The effect was more modest but still looked intentional. I stood up and nearly fell over as my foot tangled in the hem of the flowing skirt.

"That is a problem." Ena glanced over at Deirdre, and the fox disappeared into a trunk again. She emerged a moment later with a large pair of sewing scissors in her mouth, the handles shaped like a feathered bird.

"It will be quicker if you do the trimming. We don't have any thumbs." Ena nodded at the scissors as Deirdre dropped them at my feet. Slowly, their meaning sank in.

"You want me to hack off the bottom of this dress?" I squeaked. "But it's so pretty! That must be hand-embroidered."

"Yes, yes, but we can't have you tripping down the hallway to dinner." Deirdre said something, and Ena nodded. "We'll have a few dresses altered for you, but for tonight, the scissors. Right above the trim should be perfect."

I sighed and knelt in a pouf of skirts and resigned myself to crimes against haute couture. I did my best to cut an even line around the whole skirt and the underskirt as well, but it wouldn't stand up to close scrutiny. On the other hand, when I got up I didn't fall over my feet, so there was that.

"Quick, quick, sit down," huffed Ena, gesturing to a low, padded stool. I sat, and the little fox scampered up on a trunk behind me. I'd never had my hair done by a thumbless forest creature before, and it was almost embarrassing how much better than me she was at it. She tutted at my bed head and braided my hair into a soft crown woven through with blue ribbons and strung with pearls. When I stood up and looked in the mirror again, I was transformed.

"Perfect." Deirdre's voice was sweet and heavily accented. She gave my hair a satisfied pat.

"Almost perfect." Ena passed Deirdre a handful of gold and flashing blue gems.

Deirdre draped the necklace around my neck and fastened the clasp. "You're right. That's exactly what she needed."

"I can't wear this." I touched the largest gem gingerly. I could have sworn it hummed a little under my finger. "These look like sapphires! They must be worth a fortune."

"Oh, it's not like you're running off with them." Ena brushed off my concerns. "It's only for dinner. Now, there's no time for the leipreacháns to make you slippers tonight so this will have to do." Ena's tone suggested she was more satisfied than her words let on. A clock chimed in the hallway. "And just in time for dinner. Follow me."

"Thank you!" I called to Deirdre as Ena herded me out the door. The little fox bobbed her head and continued tidying up the shorn scraps of fabrics.

As I followed the raccoon down the hallway, I grew increasingly nervous. Sure, I had rescued the bear prince, but I'd also run back into the wolves and nearly gotten him killed first. Not that it was my fault for panicking. Talking raccoons aside, he had been a rather frightening sight. I tried to distract myself from my nerves by focusing on my surroundings. We descended the staircase I had escaped down yesterday...or was it this morning?...and I trailed my hand down the rich wood banister. The floors and occasional bits of rich furniture were spotless, but their neatness was offset by the cobwebs in the upper corners. Who kept the castle tidy? Were they hopping around with dusters in their teeth?

We paused in front of a tall arched doorway to the left of the main entrance. I gathered my courage and stepped into the dining hall. It was impressive. A glittering chandelier hung over a long wooden table, much too large for two people. While the table wasn't covered with food, mercifully, there was still a mouthwatering feast with some sort of roast bird in the middle and fruit, rolls, and covered dishes surrounding it. I could see the setting sun through the windows, but the room was cozily lit with candles and the chandelier. But I barely noticed any of that as he stood to greet me.

The bear had shaved off his beard, revealing high cheekbones and a strong face that appeared far younger than I had expected. He didn't look more than a couple of years older than me, although with magic in the equation I had no idea what that meant. The prince's ragged clothes had been replaced with a tailored vest and long coat that reminded me of something out of a Jane Austen movie. If Mr. Darcy wore black, with black, and a bit of black.

His dark brown hair looked like it had been hacked off at his shoulders with a knife, but it was neatly tied back, revealing slightly pointed ears. His ravaged eye was covered with a leather eye patch, but the scars around it were still clearly visible. He was no less imposing for being cleaned up as he towered at the end of the table, and even with the scars, he was shockingly handsome.

The food smelled delicious, and my stomach grumbled loudly into the silence, reminding me to get on with the eating part of the evening. I made my way to the empty place setting, feeling a bit silly in my bare feet.

The prince's good eye widened as I approached, and it didn't appear to be from appreciation.

"Where," he said through clenched teeth, "did you get that necklace?"

"I— I— I'm not sure?" I took a step back as his nostrils flared in anger. "Ena found it for me and..."

"Ena!" I swear the chandelier shook a little from the force of his bellow. The raccoon scampered in and sat calmly by my feet.

"Sir?"

"Why is she wearing Neala's necklace?" His words were punctuated by a fist on the table that rattled the dishes and made me jump.

"I suppose you'd rather have her come to dinner adorned with mud and twigs like a Grogoch?" Ena said with a sniff. "That's all she had when she arrived."

A low growl started in his throat. I'd had about enough for one evening. I could just leave, but I was really, very hungry, and the food looked too good to ignore. The bear and the raccoon kept on arguing about Neala, who—

ever that was. Well, he raged, and she calmly did not apologize.

I ignored them and grabbed a plate, loading it up with meat and vegetables. The roasted bird looked a bit small for chicken. Maybe it was a pheasant?

"It's not as though she has need of a necklace anymore, my lord," said Ena softly. A vein pulsed in the bear's forehead. His attention swung back to me as I snuck toward the doorway.

"Where are you going?!" he bellowed. "Sit down."

I bristled at his tone. "No."

He blinked.

"I don't know what you're so upset about, but I'm pretty sure it has nothing to do with me, and this is not how I'm going to spend my evening. If I'd wanted to be yelled at, I could have stayed in the comfort of my own home and been yelled at there. Do you think I care about gems and finery? Formal dinners?" I clumsily undid the necklace with one hand and tossed it at his face. Sadly, his reflexes were faster than mine, and he snatched it out of the air before it hit him. "I'm taking this back to my room." I brandished my plate in the air.

"We're having a nice dinner. I shaved!"

"And your cheekbones are fantastic. Have a lovely evening!" And with that, I fled, stealing another pastry off the end of the table as I left. For dessert.

I thought he might follow me, but as I left, I heard his voice echoing through the doorway.

"Wait, what room did you put her in?!"
One with a lock, I hoped.

A little while later, when my hands had stopped shaking, I changed out of the princess dress and back into the white nightgown. I might have sounded bold, but I sure didn't feel it. I had left home, and here I was, running away from conflict again. And no book or headphones to escape with here. I crawled up onto my bed and munched on my faerie take-out meal. It was cooler here than it had been at home. Someone had come in and closed my windows and lit a fire in the corner fireplace while I was being yelled at for no reason.

Would I be going home soon? If it was nighttime here, was it morning at home? Maybe I should change back into my own clothes. But where were they? I hadn't seen them since my bath, leaving me with no trace of my normal life.

My thoughts were troubled, but the pheasant was ridiculously good, and I was shamelessly licking my fingers clean when I heard a knock at the door.

Too much force to be a raccoon. I glared at the door.

"You don't have to open the door, *Àlainn*, I just…" He let out a grumpy sigh that was not unlike the noise he might have made as a bear. I slid off my bed with a grumble and brought my plate over to the door. I considered

71

opening it, but I didn't really want to see him. And besides, I was in my nightgown. I sat down in front of the door instead and selected a pastry from the plate.

"You just?" I prompted, taking a bite. The pastry practically melted in my mouth, all buttery flakes surrounding some sort of raspberry center. Those beavers in the kitchen knew their stuff.

"I apologize. For before. I'm not used to guests, and…" He paused, clearly at a loss. "I was caught off guard. It won't happen again."

"Who's necklace was it?"

"What's your name?"

I just glared at the wooden door, popping another pastry into my mouth.

"I hope you will have dinner with me tomorrow," he continued, as if I hadn't asked a question. "I promise to be on my best behavior."

"You know that's not an answer."

"I'll answer your questions when you answer mine. I'll see you at dinner tomorrow. I have business to attend to during the day, but feel free to explore the castle. I'm sure Ena can find someone to show you around."

"I'm not going home yet?" I tried to sound casual.

"It's still not safe, I'm afraid. Time moves more slowly in your world."

"Then, can I go outside? I don't want to stumble into any wolf packs." I gazed sadly at the crumbs on my empty plate. No more pastry.

"The Rose Gate is the only way back to your world. You may explore the castle grounds if you like. Nothing will hurt you here."

"What happens if I leave the grounds?"

"You can't."

"What kind of answer is that? Why can't I? When can I go home?"

"Good night, *Àlainn*. See you at dinner." Before I could ask any more questions, I heard his footsteps fading down the hall.

"Goodnight, Bear," I told the closed door. I climbed back up into bed, but I lay there staring at the glowing fireplace for a long time before sleep claimed me.

CHAPTER 8

WHERE WAS THAT SCRATCHING NOISE coming from? I pried one eye open and tried to wake up. Was it the door?

"Come in!" With a yawn, I sat up and rubbed my eyes.

My room was still dark, but the morning light was doing its best to invade the cracks around the heavy velvet curtains. The scratching continued and I grumbled under my breath as I felt my way over to the doorway, pausing to brush crumbs off my foot as I stepped in the plate I had left there. Apparently, you still needed to pick up after yourself in magic castles. I opened the door a crack, and instead of Ena or Deirdre, a sleek, gray-striped cat slipped in. It twined around my bare ankles before it hopped up onto my bed and settled in to lick its leg. Huh.

"Good morning?" Was this another transformed faerie? The cat paused to look at me, then went back to its grooming. I was still blinking at it and contemplating whether sliding back into bed would be rude when I heard a small rap at my partially opened door. I went back to greet a small menagerie as Ena pushed her way in with a cheery greeting. Deirdre and a little otter followed her in, carrying a basket between them.

"Breakfast!" trilled Ena as she pulled a long cord to open the curtains. Morning people.

I blinked as the room flooded with light. Deirdre hopped up onto the chair by the fireplace, and the otter passed her up a place setting complete with a linen napkin and an assortment of food to set on the little table. There was a tricky moment with a small teapot, but they managed without spilling a drop.

"This is Tait." Ena waved a paw at the otter, who was settling down near the table. "He does odd jobs around the castle. When we can find him, that is."

Tait examined his paws.

"Do sit, my dear." Ena patted the chair as Deirdre scampered off to my closet.

I sat. It looked glorious. Sausages, some sort of eggy-looking pastry, sliced melon, and a steaming cup of dark tea with a small dish of honey beside it.

"Don't you want any?" I asked the enchanted servants.

The otter stared at the sausages with a mournful expression.

"Oh, aren't you sweet?" Ena clucked. "We ate breakfast an hour ago, don't you worry."

"And, um, Cat? Are you hungry?"

The cat purred happily and settled down for a nap.

"Oh, Rani's a good mouser. I wouldn't worry about her." Ena finished opening the second set of curtains and hopped up onto the window seat to open the windows a crack and let the morning breeze drift in.

"So she's not an enchanted faerie cat?" I stirred a generous teaspoon of honey into my cup and sipped the tea. It was strong and piping hot. Perfection.

"Oh, dear me, no, simply a cat. She showed up at the castle a couple of years ago. Cats do what they like, you know."

I eyed Rani as she yawned and tucked her chin on her outstretched paws. Apparently, what she liked was my bed. I'd never had a pet. My mother hadn't been fond of things that left hair on her clothes.

I ate my breakfast and slowly began to feel more human as the tea worked its caffeinated magic on me. Deirdre popped out of my closet, daintily dragging a mint green dress behind her and up onto the bed. How long had these faeries been cursed? They seemed quite efficient in animal form.

Once I finished, the otter and Deirdre reversed their earlier performance and tucked the dishes and the remains of my breakfast back into the basket. Tait smoothly snuck a leftover sausage when Deirdre wasn't looking.

"Take the basket back to the kitchen, Tait, if you please," ordered Ena. "And then come back here directly. I have another job for you this morning."

Tait, cheeks suspiciously full, just nodded and pulled the basket out of the room, pausing to swing the small door shut with his tail on the way out.

"This one today, I think," said Deirdre in her soft, accented voice, patting the minty pile of cloth on my bed.

I shook the dress out and found it to be much simpler than the gown I'd worn to dinner the night before. It was light and soft with short sleeves and embroidered flowers along the hem. I slipped out of my nightgown and pulled the dress over my head. It was probably meant to fall a couple of inches below the knee on its original owner, the mysterious Neala, but on me it hit mid-calf.

Deirdre directed me to turn, and deftly tightened the laces up the back with gentle tugs of paws and teeth. I shook my head. This was the strangest morning of my life, but as the dress swished around my legs, I had to admit it was pretty fun to play dress-up in a castle with a fox for a lady's maid.

In the gleaming bathroom, I washed my face in the white stone sink and brushed my hair before Deirdre entered with a mint ribbon in her mouth and directed me to sit on a cushion.

"I can just put it in a ponytail," I protested, but the little fox gave me such a look that I sat. She tied the ribbon around my head and braided the back up into some sort of pretty knot I would never be able to replicate.

When we were back in the bedroom, Ena opened the door for Tait, who had returned from the kitchen. "Now, Deirdre and I must get to our daily tasks, but Tait here has agreed to take some time out of his busy schedule of avoiding work and swimming in the pond..."

Tait fixed his eyes on the ceiling. Clearly, he was the picture of innocence.

"...to be your guide around the castle. Come by the kitchen around noon for lunch—don't worry, Tait won't be likely to miss a meal—and you'll have dinner with the prince again tonight."

Another dinner with the bear. I quelled my sense of apprehension. Plucking at my dress, I wondered about its previous owner. Who was she to cause such a violent reaction from him? Or maybe he just liked to yell.

"Ena?"

The little raccoon turned back to look at me from the doorway. "Yes?"

"Do you know how long I have to stay here? I mean..." I was coming across as a little ungrateful. "...you've all been lovely." The master of the house excepted. "But do you know when it will be daytime in my world?"

"You'll have to ask the master at dinner. The time difference isn't constant, and I don't pay much attention to it. I rarely leave the castle. He'll be keeping an eye on it for you."

"Oh, okay. Thanks, Ena." Even though I knew time was moving slowly in the human world, I couldn't help but think of my family worrying about me being gone all night. Well, Lily would worry anyway. She'd be sure a bear had gotten me out in the woods, after all. Which wasn't untrue, come to think of it.

"I know it's all a bit strange, but try to enjoy your time here. We're more than happy to have someone to fuss over."

I tried to imagine them fussing over the bear and couldn't see him putting up with it.

"Off you go with Tait now. We'll see you in the kitchen for lunch." She gave the otter a stern look. "Be on your best behavior, lad."

"Yes, Ena," he said humbly, before adding under his breath to me, "You're lucky she's not the one giving you the tour. You'd never see anything interesting."

I wasn't sure whether to be encouraged or worried as I followed the little otter out the door.

CHAPTER 9

TAIT MIGHT HAVE BEEN QUIET AROUND ENA, for whom he clearly had a healthy respect, but he turned quite chatty as he led me around. As interesting as it was to be in an enchanted castle, I asked him to show me around the grounds. It was too nice to be inside. The day was beautiful, more like a crisp autumn day than the dry heat I had left behind. Hmm. It might actually be autumn here. I wasn't sure how it all worked.

We started with the front garden, which I'd seen briefly as I fled through it the day before. On closer inspection it was lovely, with formal hedges lining the wide gravel path that led to the Rose Gate. The hedges were neatly trimmed to waist height and swirled off maze-like to line fanciful paths that hid benches and flower beds.

I first wanted to examine the Rose Gate more closely, so I walked down the main path with Tait scampering along behind me. I stopped short of the gate, not wanting to accidentally stumble into a wolf pack again. The smell of the roses in the sun surrounded me, and I brushed one deep red flower gently with a finger. It was the same type of rose I had seen growing near the miner's cabin.

I could feel a faint hum again, deep in my bones, but other than that, the roses here didn't seem to be behaving strangely. Beautiful, but completely normal with their petals opened wide to the sun. The gate was wider than I could reach with my arms stretched out, and the rose-covered stone arch was higher than I could touch even with a jump. Two people on horses could probably ride through it without touching. Or a minivan.

Through the gate I could see the dirt trail and forest I'd thought were the way home as I dashed toward the gate yesterday, but now I could clearly see that it was a different forest altogether. The trail was actually a faint road, wide enough for a carriage, and the massive trees towered above a mossy forest floor covered with tiny flowers and mushrooms. A faerie forest.

I wanted to explore it, but I knew stepping through the gate would only take me back to the wolves.

"I visited the clearing with the cabin twice the night I came here," I said. "That must be where the gate leads. The roses are the same. Why did I never come through to Faerie?"

"It's the magic of the gate," piped up Tait. "You can't pass through without permission from the lord or lady of the castle."

"I guess they don't want humans stumbling through it any old time," I said.

"Not just humans. No one can go through it. How do you think those wolves are kept out?"

Something to be grateful for.

"Those wolves. They aren't normal wolves, are they?"

"Nope," Tait responded cheerily. "They're minions of the Unseelie Queen." His voice dropped to a dramatic whisper. "She collects the most handsome young men as her pets. Wolves by night, faeries by day. Doing her evil bidding until their last breath."

"Is that who cursed the castle? The Unseelie Queen?"

"I said no such thing," protested Tait. "Be sure to mention I didn't...if it comes up."

"And yet, you're an otter? Not handsome enough to be turned into a wolf?"

"I'm sure she didn't get a good look at me," the otter grumbled. "Have you stared at the roses long enough yet?"

I watched the roses a minute more to see if they were planning on doing anything interesting. Nope. Time to move on.

One side path on the left led to a fountain of carved white stone. A tall, graceful lady stood in the middle with wings folded down her back, pouring water out of a jug on her shoulder. At her feet sat all sorts of strange little carved figures, some beautiful and some disturbing, with wings and horns. Near the bottom, tiny mermaids with sharp teeth lounged at the edge of the water.

"What sort of faerie were you, Tait? Before you were enchanted, I mean."

Tait slipped into the little pool surrounding the fountain and eyed the little darting fish with great interest.

"I'm a phouka, lady." He splashed under the water and came up munching a little goldfish with an air of satisfaction.

"What's a phouka?" I tried to remember, but my faerie knowledge was pretty spotty.

"A shape-shifter," he said around a bite of fish. "Don't believe anything you've heard about us. The rumors are greatly exaggerated."

"They're nothing but mischief, they are," twittered a little gray bird overhead.

"Don't let Geanan catch you eating the goldfish!" sang a little yellow bird before sailing off.

"All the animals here aren't faeries? Are they?" I asked Tait. Should I be concerned about the fish he'd just finished off?

"Oh no." He jumped up onto the fountain's edge and shook himself off, spraying me with little drops of water. "The curse turned all the faeries into animals, but the animals that were already here stayed animals."

"How do you tell them apart?" I asked, not completely reassured.

"Oh, we know who we are."

"Well then, how can I tell you all apart?" I looked up at the birds flying around the garden.

"Er, say hi?" He shrugged. "Come on. I'll show you the back garden. The pond there is much nicer."

"Do you mind? Being an otter, I mean?" I followed Tait's wet paw prints around the path that circled the castle.

"Hmm, I do miss being able to shape-shift." He gave a liquid ottery shrug. "But I always liked swimming, so it's not too bad. At least I'm not a bug or something. Watch your step!"

I froze, suddenly wary of stepping on a beetle and ending some little faerie's life. Tait snorted with suppressed laughter, and I gave him a narrowed look. Mischief indeed.

***

After a tour of the back garden, which contained fewer hedges and more carrots and tomatoes than the front garden, Tait and I popped into the kitchen for lunch. A beaver gave us a basket, which we took out through the kitchen's back door. Sitting on the sun-warmed stone steps, we ate boiled eggs, cheese, and fresh rolls. Tait finished all his food before I was even done with my first egg and proceeded to hunt around the bottom of the steps for small creatures to eat.

I surveyed the view as I ate. Beyond the steps was a large kitchen garden, a couple of rows of fruit trees, and beyond them, a small pasture with shaggy, horned cows. Chickens ran loose all over the garden area, and bees droned in the orchard. Clearly all the delicious food I'd been enjoying grew right here. There was a low stone wall between the garden and the pasture. What was beyond the animals? I squinted, but the horizon refused to come into focus. I could see a few haystacks, and then it was just blurry like the background of an artistic photo or the haze of heat in the desert.

"What's past the cow pasture?" I kept squinting. It seemed like I should be able to see it if I tried hard enough.

"More cow pasture, I think," said Tait around a mouthful of frog.

"Why can't I see it? Why's it so blurry?"

"Oh, that's the edge." He continued to munch.

"The edge of what?"

"The edge of the curse," he said, with an unspoken *obviously*.

My pulse picked up. I knew there was a curse, but this was the first I'd heard about a physical border being involved.

"Show me," I said, getting to my feet and brushing crumbs off my dress.

Tait looked conflicted—a serious look for someone with a frog's leg sticking out of his mouth. How many instructions had he been given regarding where I was supposed to go and what he should tell me? I made the decision easy for him and started off toward the field, snagging an apple from a tree on my way past. I'd never eaten an apple off the tree before, and I was momentarily distracted by the explosion of sweet flavor.

"You've ruined me for grocery store apples," I told the fruit sadly.

Tait caught up to me, and I went through the wooden gate, latched it behind me, and strode into the pasture. I gave a wide berth to the cows, which were rather large when you got right up to them, and the giant horns were a bit off-putting. One turned a large brown eye my way, and I took a nervous step back.

"Watch your feet!" called Tait, and I narrowly avoided a steaming puddle of giant cow poo.

"Are cows meant to be this size?" I eyed the cows. I had admittedly not spent much time on farms, but I was relatively sure that a cow was smaller than a rhinoceros.

"They're aurochs, not cows. Maybe you should come back before I—I mean we—get into trouble."

"What's an auroch?" I gave the nearest giant, furry cow another nervous glance as I continued toward the edge of the pasture.

"They're the ancestors of your cows. I think. I'm an otter, not a dairy farmer."

"Hmm." The aurochs seemed content to graze. I picked my way carefully between them until I was across the small field and had reached the edge of the pasture. I could feel that strange buzzing feeling, like with the roses. The buzzing grew stronger as I got closer. From close up, the out-of-focus view was much stranger. I could see that the sky was blue, and there was a vague impression of a matching field with some dark patches here and there, but nothing clearer than that. I finished my apple and threw the core at the wall of blur. It arced into the air and blurred into a hazy shadow when it passed through the curse's edge.

Curious, I took a step forward and reached out my hand.

"Wait, don't do tha—" Tait's warning echoed as I plunged into darkness. The emptiness pressed in around me, pushing the air out of my lungs. I could hear screaming growing steadily louder and louder. It was the voice of a terrified woman, and I wondered distantly if it was me screaming, but I couldn't even draw enough breath to gasp.

Help me, help me, help me, please, I begged silently, unable to step back to the pasture or even move a finger. I was on the verge of total panic when a warm hand grasped mine, and I was jerked back to the cow pasture.

I tumbled backward, gasping for air in short, panicked breaths. I shook my head to clear it. The bear prince held me upright. The world tipped sideways, and he caught me against him and lowered us both to sit on the ground. I should have pulled back, but I needed a moment to be sure I wouldn't fall over.

"Breathe, *Àlainn*," ordered the prince. He ran a hand down my back, and I took a deep shaking breath. He turned to Tait. The otter winced.

"Tait!" the bear roared. "What were you thinking?"

"I'm sorry, my lord! I didn't think she'd..." He hung his head. "Sorry! I'll go back to the kitchens and clean something."

The bear gave a low growl, and Tait scampered back through the field.

"It's not his fault." Now that I'd gotten my breath back, I realized I was practically in the prince's lap. I pulled myself back to put a few more inches between us. "I was curious. I didn't know that would happen."

"Don't touch the edge," the prince rumbled.

"No, I don't think I will," I gasped, my body still shaking. I took another deep breath. "What does it mean? The edge of the curse? What's beyond it?"

He stared at the stone wall in the distance, clearly debating what to tell me. "The rest of Faerie," he said at last. "That's what's beyond the edge. The curse has cut us off from Tír na nÓg. The only way left to leave the castle is the Rose Gate. And the Rose Gate now only leads to your world."

I stared at the edge. "So, you're trapped here." He said nothing. "But what is the curse exactly?"

He ignored my question and helped me to my feet.

We stood there, my hand still in his, and a million questions ran through my mind. Before I could open my mouth, his gaze dropped from mine, and he abruptly let go and turned back to the castle.

"Try to stay out of trouble until dinnertime," he called over his shoulder as he strode across the golden field.

I made a face at his back, but a witty retort eluded me, especially as he was right. I gave one more look to the blurred edge of the bubble that surrounded us, and then I shivered and turned as well. I quickly darted between the calmly grazing aurochs back to the castle, happy to have more distance between me and that screaming darkness.

CHAPTER 10

THAT NIGHT DEIRDRE DRESSED ME IN DEEP blue with little golden stars. I gave a twirl in front of the mirror. Star-tipped golden pins shone against my dark hair, and the effect was of a princess of the night sky. It seemed like rather a lot of work just to prepare for a dinner with someone who might decide to either ignore me or yell at me, but I kept my opinion to myself. I didn't want Ena and Deirdre to think I was ungrateful, and they seemed to be having fun.

Today's dress fit perfectly. Had little animals spent the day working on it like something out of a Disney movie? Probably. Soft-soled shoes of buttery charcoal leather completed the outfit. Maybe they'd let me take them when I went home. My designer ballet flats had nothing on these.

Ena led me past mysterious doors and stairwells on the way to the dining room. I needed to explore the castle more thoroughly tomorrow, if I was still here.

I paused outside the dining room.

"Don't you worry, my dear. He'll behave tonight," Ena assured me.

"Hmmm," I replied. But there was nothing to gain by standing in the hallway, so I pretended a confidence I didn't feel and entered the dining room.

The glowing chamber looked much like it had the night before, with the table covered in mouthwatering food and the man seated at it in formal black.

The prince rose as I entered, and I narrowed my eyes, waiting to see what he would make of my appearance today. While he didn't exactly look happy—had I ever seen him smile? Maybe there was something wrong with his teeth—he didn't growl either. He walked over and took my hand in his with a slight bow and then led me to the table.

"So formal," I said once we were both seated. I fiddled with my collection of forks and wondered if there were cutlery police hiding somewhere. Maybe a mouse would pop up from behind the fruit bowl and scold me if I used the wrong spoon.

"The cooks are pleased to have someone around to appreciate their talents." He passed me a plate of meat.

"You don't usually eat like this?" Considering his scraggly appearance when we first met, it was hard to imagine he bothered with formal dinners.

"There doesn't seem to be much point, eating in here alone." He continued dishing up in silence, then added, "Often, I eat as a bear. It seems simpler, but it makes Ena exasperated."

Had he always lived here with just the staff, or did he have a family before the curse? I was pretty sure, given our track record, that if I asked, he would choose to ignore me.

"What were you so busy with today?" I asked instead.

"When I wasn't rescuing overly curious humans who feel the need to touch cursed boundary lines, I was checking the flow of time in your world to see when it will be safe for you to go home."

Touché.

"And?" I took a sip of water in an attempt to look casual. How was he checking the flow of time? And what did that even mean?

"It's hard to pinpoint the exact hour, but I would guess you'll be safest here for around a fortnight." He carefully did not meet my eyes, but instead took a bite of food.

"What?!" I sputtered, spraying water out of my mouth in a *very* ladylike fashion.

"About fourteen days," he said helpfully. "Give or take."

"I know what a fortnight is!" My voice began to rise. "I read Jane Austen!"

"Er, alright then."

"I cannot stay here for two weeks," I said, although a treacherous part of me thought it wouldn't mind a couple of weeks with princess dresses and mysterious castles. "I have...things. And stuff. To do!"

"I understand your family might be concerned, but almost no time will pass in your world. Think of it like a holiday," he suggested.

"I didn't want to take a holiday!"

"Anytime you decide being eaten by wolves is preferable, you know where the portal is."

I took a deep breath and convinced myself that smacking the smug look off the bear's face would cause more trouble than it was worth. Maybe.

"What am I supposed to do for two weeks? Catch goldfish with Tait? I don't even have my books."

"Has Tait been eating the goldfish again? Geanan will not be happy when he finds out."

I stabbed at a roasted vegetable viciously.

"What sort of books do you like?" He wisely ignored my carrot decapitation.

"Oh, I don't know, all sorts of things." I poked at a potato morosely. "Mostly fiction. Romance. Vampires. Whatever." I didn't add fairy tales, or he would be back to convincing me that this was a dreamy holiday.

The bear barked with laughter. When I glared at him, he explained, "If your human authors met the Dearg-due, they wouldn't be writing romances about them."

"I was supposed to be reading them from the ignorant safety of my bedroom, thank you very much."

He sobered at that.

"I am sorry, *Àlainn*. I wouldn't have brought you here if it hadn't been the only way."

"Are you going to tell me what that name means yet?" I grumbled.

"You could tell me your real name, and I'll use it instead."

"Well, are you going to tell me yours?"

The bear just smiled and started back on his meal. And with a sigh, so did I.

Later that night when I was back in my bedroom watching the flames dance in the fireplace with Rani on my lap, I heard the noise of something sliding under my door. I tipped the cat off my lap and went to investigate. On the ground was a beautiful leather-bound book with embossed swirls and gilt lettering that read *The Fenian Cycle*.

Rani sniffed the book and proclaimed it boring with a chirrup before stalking back to the fireside chair. When I opened the heavy book, a scrap of paper fluttered out. I caught it and read the note. It was written in a much neater script than anyone in the land of emails and texting could manage.

Alainn, I hope you enjoy this book. It was one of my favorites growing up.
Yours, Leith

CHAPTER 11

T HE NEXT MORNING TAIT HELPED deliver my breakfast, but when I asked him if he'd help me explore the castle, he mumbled something indistinct and scurried off with the basket.

"Why can't Tait show me around?" I asked Ena as Deirdre fussed over my hair. Today's day dress was dove gray with white stripes. It seemed Neala had preferred a wardrobe in cool tones. I liked a bit more pop to my wardrobe personally, but beggars couldn't be choosers.

Ena laughed. "Geanan found out about the goldfish and is making Tait help in the gardens for a few days where he can keep an eye on him."

"A little bird told him?" I guessed.

"Precisely. The goldfish population needs to be carefully maintained as we have no way of getting more if Tait eats them all."

I remembered the blurred barrier and shivered.

"Maybe I could bring some from my world. From the pet store, I mean. Do you think they're any different from faerie goldfish?" I hadn't considered much past what I would do when I left the castle, but the words were out of my mouth before I thought about it. Maybe I could come back and visit. Make sure Tait didn't get into too much trouble.

Ena gave me an unreadable look...but really, what did I know about raccoon expressions? "I'm sure Geanan would appreciate that. As far as I've seen, creatures from the human world seem to get along just fine in Faerie."

"What about humans?" I asked, suddenly curious. "Do humans ever live in Faerie?"

"Hmm, not often out in the countryside. There are more at the courts, although not always of their own free will. The *Tuatha Dé Danann* will steal away a human from time to time, if they have a talent for music or art the fae find interesting. They are treated with honor, but never released until their captor tires of them."

I shivered, imagining how worried my family would be if I was truly trapped here. Ena patted my hand with her paw.

"Not to worry, my dear, things aren't like that at Kilinaire. You'll be on your way home soon enough."

I nodded. While I sometimes felt like I'd been trapped here, I didn't truly believe Leith meant to keep me prisoner. I silently watched Deirdre in the mirror as she finished braiding my hair back in some sort of soft and simple-looking tail I would never in a thousand years be able to replicate. She wound a gray ribbon around the bottom and gave a little cluck as the ribbon tied itself around my hair.

"Wait. How did you do that?" I had been wondering how she managed such complicated hairstyles with little fox paws. I should have guessed there was magic involved.

"Oh, it's only a small magic." She tucked a stray bit of hair into the braid. "Keeps your hair in place for the day."

That explained why my hair had been so well-behaved since I arrived at Kilinaire. I touched the ribbon gingerly with my fingers. It didn't feel any different than a normal ribbon.

"When you tug the ribbon, the spell comes undone."

"That's amazing!" I told her. "I didn't know you could do magic! Can all faeries?"

"Oh, it's nothing much."

"Anyone can do small magic." Ena gathered up my nightgown. "It's merely a use of the natural magic all around us. Only a powerful faerie can do great magic or create magical objects."

"Like the curse?" I was eager for any more details I could gather.

"The curse," she said carefully, "is neither small magic nor great magic. It's blood magic."

A shiver went down my spine.

"What is the curse, Ena?" I asked gently.

"It's not my story to tell you, is what it is." She nodded briskly to Deirdre and they headed for the door. "Now, feel free to go where you wish this morning, but I would stay out of the back tower if I were you."

"Oh?" I tried not to perk up at the warning. "What's in the back tower?" Would it contain clues to the castle's mysteries?

Ena laughed. "The Prince's living quarters. I wouldn't wander in without an invitation."

Or maybe not.

And so, I spent my morning poking around the castle. It was quite evident the stately home wasn't as full as it had been designed to be. I found sections locked and boarded off, with others covered in thick layers of dust. The upper floor, which held the bedrooms, was especially empty. Only the wing containing my suite was clean and bright. Why had those rooms been kept up when there was no one living in this part of the castle anymore?

As far as I could tell there were three ways to travel between the castle floors. The corner towers each held a narrow, spiral staircase. The lack of headroom on those stairs proved that they were mainly used for the staff to travel through the castle without bothering anyone. This was how I'd been traveling from the ground floor to the kitchen. Honestly, the builder's assumption that all the servants were short was a bit disturbing. The superiority of the tall *Tuatha Dé Danann* was clearly so ingrained in the culture that the architecture reflected it.

Next there was the grand staircase that I had been up and down between my rooms and dinner, all white stone with plush carpet down the middle. When I stood at the top, I peeked over a carved wooden railing and saw the castle's entranceway. Halfway down the stairs was a wide landing with a gallery of paintings. The last way of navigating the castle would be the back tower, which had a locked doorway on every floor. Don't ask me how I knew they were locked.

The castle was intriguing but also a bit lonely. While it was nice to get away from the constant noise of living in such close quarters with my sisters, the castle felt echoingly silent. During my exploration, I didn't cross paths with anyone but a pair of spotted rabbits. They appeared out of a small doorway in the upstairs hallway with rags to polish the bits of occasional furniture, ignoring me completely. Clearly there were even more ways to navigate the castle when you were only eight inches high. What had all the inhabitants of Kilinaire looked like before the mysterious curse fell upon them?

That afternoon, happily full from my lunch on the back step with Tait, I found my way back to the gallery of paintings. I had brought my book, but it was closed in my lap while I sat on a velvet-upholstered bench considering a portrait that caught my eye. I didn't know a great deal about art, but these paintings were all clearly masterpieces. Across from me, so real I half expected them to blink, were Leith and a beautiful fae lady. Her delicately pointed ears poked out from hair that was a lighter brown than Leith's and streaked with gold, but there was something similar about their eyes, and they shared the same high cheekbones. She held a cat that looked suspiciously like Rani.

The Leith in the painting was…not exactly younger, but softer. Not that he was smiling, heaven forbid, but his clear gray eyes looked less troubled, his face unscarred, his jaw unclenched.

I heard footsteps come down the corridor, and the real Leith appeared as if called by my thoughts and sat down beside me on the bench. We sat there in silence looking at the painting together, not touching, but close enough that I could feel him next to me.

"You used to wear your hair short." I picked the safest comment I could find.

He sighed and ran a hand through his unruly hair. "I did. I prefer it short under a helm. But I have no one to cut it for me now." He paused for a long moment. "I suppose I also have no one to fight. The length of my hair doesn't matter much when I'm a bear, but it is a bit annoying when I'm myself."

"Were you a warrior then?" I tapped the book on my lap with a note of teasing in my voice. "Like Fionn mac Cumhail and the Fianna?"

"Fionn retired long before I joined them, but yes, I was a warrior in one of the King's Fianna for a time."

"What?" I squeaked. "Are these stories all true then?" I eyed the book suspiciously. I had been sure it contained Irish folk tales.

"They are, and they aren't. Fionn mac Cumhail was real, and while some of the stories are greatly exaggerated, they're based on truth. His fame was such that he caught the eye of Fiachra, the Seelie King. Fiachra brought him and a handful of his warriors to Tír na nÓg to train his own war band."

"Which you were a warrior in?" He didn't seem old enough to have already been a soldier, a warrior in a fabled fianna, and have moved on.

"Once upon a time." Leith's attention was still on the younger version of himself or perhaps the young woman painted next to him.

"The likeness is amazing. Do faerie painters use magic?" I asked.

"The artist used a spell to keep the colors from fading and doubtless some other tricks to keep the paint wet or dry it at will. But the skill isn't magic. Faerie artists live longer than human artists, so they have more time to re-fine their talents."

"How much longer?" I sized up the youthful-looking fae man beside me. "How old are you, anyway?"

"We get a little over ten years for every one of yours," he told me. "And it's not polite to ask."

I thought about this. I'd get his age out of him later. "Do faerie animals live longer too? What about faerie cats, like Rani?" I wondered if Tait was in trouble for eating an immortal goldfish.

"Yes. Sort of. It's not anything to do with the animals or the faeries, for that matter. It's Faerie itself. If I went to the human world, I would age as fast as any mortal there."

"And if a human came to Faerie?" I asked.

"They would live for centuries. But that rarely hap-pens. A human has to be brought to Faerie. They can't just stumble in."

Like Fionn mac Cumhail and those musicians and artists Ena had told me about. And me, apparently.

"Is that Neala?" I finally asked the question that had been burning inside me.

"Yes."

I waited to see if he was planning to elaborate. Nope.

"She was your sister." It wasn't a question, but I wanted to hear him say it.

"She was."

I thought of my sisters, worrying about me back home. They drove me crazy on an hourly basis, but I couldn't imagine losing them. "Will you tell me what happened to her? Was it part of the curse?"

"Will you tell me your name?" I heard a hint of teasing in his voice, but his face betrayed nothing.

I hesitated for a moment too long, and he continued, "Another time. It's too nice a day for such a sad story." He rose to leave, pausing in front of the painting. He ran a finger down the gilt frame before disappearing down the hall.

I watched him go and then tried to get back into my book. Even knowing they were based on truth, the stories of heroes and magic that had so enthralled me before paled in comparison to the mystery of the castle and its dead lady.

At dinner that night, I eyed the prince in amusement. He seemed a bit nervous. Maybe he was worried I would try to pick up our conversation from that afternoon. He cleared his throat.

"You must have a family," he said abruptly.

"I, um, yes." I tried to keep a straight face at his obvious attempt to distract me before I asked further questions. "I do."

"Tell me about them. Your mother must be beautiful. I mean, you must take after her. Do you?"

I took a minute to untangle what I was fairly sure was a compliment.

"My mother. Yes, she's very beautiful. And I hope my hair and my eyes are all that I've inherited from her."

He raised his eyebrows.

"My mother…she's hard to explain." I took a breath, trying to sort out my thoughts. "When my parents met, my father was a cocky investment banker, and my mother saw a handsome young man who liked to take the sort of thrilling risks that would make him a lot of money. So, she set out to marry him, and she succeeded. My oldest sister Lily was born seven months later. And my mom was right. His career did very well, and they were very rich. They didn't always get along, but they managed well enough to have me and then my little sister, Amber, so there must have been something between them still.

"I do think he loved her. She loved the idea of him. Loved having a large house to show off and loved being invited to all the best parties. She would show us off, her three beautiful girls, but once everyone was done cooing over us, she didn't notice when I escaped to my room for the night. It was Lily who read me my bedtime stories. Lily who taught Amber and me to ride our bikes, and Lily who paid attention when Amber was out too late."

"You love your sister." I could hear the loss of his own beloved sister in his voice.

"I do. I love them both, although Amber can be...prickly. But even porcupines need sisters who love them, I think." I picked up a roll and tore it in half.

"You talk about your mother as if something happened to her. Is she gone?"

"Well..." I took a breath and told myself I wouldn't cry. "Yes. She's still alive, but she's gone. Two years ago, my parents started fighting. More than the usual sniping back and forth they'd always done. They fought all the time. My dad's business was struggling, and he wanted her to cut back on her spending while he got it back on its feet."

"She didn't want to."

"He might as well have asked her to stop breathing. It simply wasn't going to happen. She was too addicted to her pretty things, and more than that, to the way people treated her because of them. She came from nothing, she always said, and she wasn't about to go back."

"From nothing?"

"That's how she saw it. It was up and down all that year. Dad's business would do better, and she would be all sweetness and light, and then the fighting would start again. The third time was the worst, when the last of the money ran out and Dad had to declare bankruptcy. She packed her bags the next morning. She kissed us each goodbye, told us we were good girls, but that we were grown up and didn't really need her anymore."

I was losing the battle with my tears now, and I'd torn my roll into tiny pieces.

"Have you seen her since then?"

"Oh, she took us out for brunch a couple of times. Showed us her new diamond. I'm pretty sure she had husband number two lined up before she even left my dad. But her new life has even less room for us than her old one did. And after we lost the house, we moved out to Pilot Bay and our old vacation cabin. It's too far from the city, she says. She's texted me once or twice. You probably don't even know what texting is..."

"I really don't," he said seriously. I sobbed out a laugh. "But I'm sorry. Not only that you lost her, but to have had such a mother in the first place."

"I know, but I can't help but wonder what might have happened if I'd tried harder to be what she wanted. To be more social. More interested in parties and... oh, I don't know, just more fun."

"This has nothing to do with you. Anyone who could leave their own daughter, who could leave you, is not seeing anyone but themselves. Trust me, you're not someone to leave."

I looked up from my mutilated roll and met the intensity of his gaze. My breath caught, and I let myself look back for longer than was wise.

"I'm sorry." I could feel my cheeks heating. "You asked a simple question. I didn't mean to bog you down with all my issues." I scrubbed my tears with my hand and pushed my chair back. "I'm not hungry tonight," I added, and for once it was the truth. My stomach was tied in knots.

He stood as well. "Good night then, *Àlainn.*"

It was all too much. I fled.

CHAPTER 12

"AND WHAT ARE YOU THINKING OF, my dear?" Ena asked the next morning as I picked at the remains of breakfast on my plate. I had been thinking about a certain growly fae prince who'd been awfully sweet at dinner last night. I was beginning to feel rather-...friendly toward him. But my opinions on the subject weren't clear enough to discuss.

"I was thinking about my day." That wasn't untrue. I couldn't spend another day wandering around and reading. Yes, shockingly, even I could get enough reading time. "Is there anything I can do to help out? You've all been so kind, but I know you didn't exactly plan to have a long-term guest."

"Oh, we love to have you," tsked Ena. "You don't know how long it's been since we've had a fresh face around here."

"Thank you, but really, is there anything I can do to help?"

"Hmm, it would be handy to have someone nice and tall around for a couple of tasks," mused the housekeeper as she opened the windows for the morning. I couldn't help a snort of laughter.

"Well, that's the first time anyone's called me tall. By human standards I'm pretty short, although I suppose I have a few inches on most forest creatures."

"You'd be considered tall by faerie standards too, my dear." Ena opened the final window and turned back to face me. "The *Tuatha Dé Danann* are quite tall, and of course there are the giants…"

"Of course," I agreed casually. Giants?

"But the rest of us come in so many different shapes and sizes that it's scarcely the first thing people notice. Myself, I wasn't much taller than a raccoon anyway. Less hairy though." She examined her paws thoughtfully.

"How long ago was that, Ena?" I was eager for any tidbits I could glean about the mysterious curse.

"Deirdre!" Ena ignored my prying, as always. The little fox poked her head out of my dressing room.

"Can you find a sturdy dress and an apron with pockets for today?"

Deirdre nodded and backed out of the room.

"The apples are in need of picking. You can help Tait for the morning. I'll show you where the ladder and wheelbarrow are after you get dressed."

"Sounds good to me." I popped the last bit of my pastry into my mouth with satisfaction. Tait had proven to be much chattier than anyone else in the castle. I'd shake the little otter up and see if I could get more than apples to drop this morning.

A half hour later, Tait and I eyed the first apple tree speculatively. It was a tall, gnarled thing with branches like witches' fingers and golden apples with blushing red cheeks.

"Sooo…" I really didn't know much about picking apples. Surely it was pretty straightforward?

"I'll climb up in the tree, if you like," said Tait, "and toss them down. You can catch them in your apron." Without waiting for an answer, the otter scurried up the tree trunk and disappeared into the leaves, reappearing a moment later along a low branch.

"Okay, spread out your apron."

"How good is your aim?" I asked cautiously.

"How good are your reflexes?" He tossed the first apple down. I managed to catch it neatly in my apron, but my smugness was short-lived as I missed the next one.

111

The third apple hit my shoulder as I crawled around looking for the second one.

"Hey! Wait a second," I protested.

Tait sighed and munched on an apple while I got myself ready for more missiles.

"Okay." I braced myself and caught three more apples before missing another one.

"I'm not sure this is actually faster than doing it myself," grumbled Tait, looking longingly through the orchard toward the fish pond.

"Do you want to wear the apron, and I'll climb up the tree?" I asked tartly.

"It couldn't be sillier than what we're currently doing. Half the apples will be bruised at this rate."

I eyed the most recently dropped fruit. It looked fine to me.

"I have an idea." I called up the tree.

"Should I be afraid?"

"Just wait a minute."

A few minutes later I was tucking my skirts up and climbing up the ladder leaning against the apple tree.

"What do you think?" I tested my weight on the branch the otter was crouching on.

He gingerly picked an apple and let it fall onto the pile of leaves I had heaped up under the tree. The apple landed softly.

"I think you're on to something! We might get this tree picked today after all."

I tugged an apple off the tree and dropped it after his.

"Try to twist it as you pull." Tait demonstrated while I watched carefully. "They keep longer if you pick them nicely. And I want apples this winter."

I twisted the next apple, and it fell off into my palm.

"Do you think the kitchen staff will make us a pie for tonight?"

"Oh, I'm sure they will if you ask," said Tait. "Although, it might depend on the amount of wheat left in storage."

"Where do you get your wheat, anyway?" I watched another apple drop down into the leaves. "You grow all your own food, right?"

"We dooo…" he said cautiously.

"But I don't see any fields for growing grain. Where do you get it?"

Tait suddenly became consumed with picking a bit of apple out of his sharp little teeth and staring up into the golden leaves.

"Super big wheat secret, is it? Black magic? Made from the blood of baby unicorns?"

Tait sighed. "I'm not supposed to talk to you about the curse. Lord Leith was very angry with me after the other day. And have you seen him angry? That throbbing vein in his forehead?"

"The snarly growls?" I supplied. "The red face?"

"Yes! Exactly! So, I'm not going to tell you anything more about the curse."

"See, but you already did." I settled down on the branch and swung my bare feet in the air, snagging another apple and biting into its tart juiciness. "Because I didn't know the wheat had anything to do with the curse. Was the castle cursed for having too many pastries? Cut off from cakes for all eternity? That does sound terrible."

"What? That's ridiculous. We just don't have wheat fields anymore."

"Aha!"

Tait winced as I poked him, but his pain seemed mainly emotional. "You *had* wheat fields, but you don't anymore, and that has to do with the curse." I stood up on the branch and held onto the tree trunk so I could lean out and eye the blurry edge of the curse past the auroch pasture.

"It moves, doesn't it? The edge of the curse. You used to have more land than you have now."

Was it closer now than it had been the other day? Surely it didn't change that quickly. I suppressed a shiver. "Tait?"

"Yes." He gave a resigned sigh. "It moves. Don't tell Lord Leith I told you anything."

"How much land did you have?" I asked softly, still eyeing the blurry horizon.

"We originally had all the castle grounds. Vast fields, a small forest, stables full of horses."

"How long have you been trapped here?" I was feeling claustrophobic just thinking about it. I couldn't imagine being here permanently.

"Oh, we can leave. We can go through the Rose Gate to your world. But we can't talk there. We're like normal animals." I imagined not being mouthy was about the worst punishment you could give a faerie like Tait. "I sometimes leave Kilinaire and go fishing in your forest-...but I don't like to stay long. I don't feel as much...myself when I'm there."

"How long?" I wasn't letting him sidestep my question that neatly.

"Nearly a century," he mumbled, reaching up for another apple.

Cursed for a hundred years. The questions piled up in my mind, but Tait suddenly froze.

"Do. Not. Move," he said very, very quietly.

"What?"

He winced at my loud question and slowly pointed out into the kitchen garden where a giant cougar stalked toward the orchard. I gripped the tree trunk tightly.

Hold still. Don't freak out.

How had it gotten through the Rose Gate? Was it some cat thing, like with Rani? It just went where it wanted to? For all my bravado when talking to Lily, I'd always been terrified of cougars. I mean, a bear will usually run away, but a cougar? They might decide to pounce on you for fun.

"He must have found out about the goldfish," whispered Tait. "I swear, I only ate a couple this time. I didn't think he'd notice!"

"Wait, what?!" I exclaimed, startled out of my panic. "That's not a real cougar?"

"His teeth are real enough." Tait shushed me. "Not that Geanan would actually eat me, but he might make me help fertilize the hedges again, and that's even worse."

I bit my lip to keep from laughing at my little friend's distress.

"Okay," I whispered, "I'll create a diversion, and you run the other way."

"What kind of diversion?"

I threw two apples, one after the other, over the herb garden and into the fish pond. One fell short, but the other landed with a satisfying splash. Geanan turned his head toward the noise.

"Go, go, go!" I whispered urgently as Tait jumped out of the tree, landing gracefully beside the apples.

"I owe you one," the otter called as he scampered through the apple trees.

The cougar stalked off around to the other side of the castle, and I was left alone with a pile of apples and an even bigger heap of questions.

"What do you think of the pie?" I asked Leith later that night as he took seconds of dessert. I was pretty dang proud of it. I'd never baked a pie before, and it had taken some persistent harassing of Ena and the beaver pastry chef before I'd gotten my way and been taught how.

The pie crust had some patchwork in the bottom of the pan, but it was light and flaky, and the spiced apples tasted incredible. I'd have to show off my new skills to Lily when I got home.

"It's very...good?" Leith eyed me warily. Perhaps he was worried that I'd slipped something into his dessert to pay him back for refusing to answer any of my questions. But that's not how I roll. I'm not that subtle.

"Thank you. I think so too. Speaking of pies, why did you tell T——the staff——that they couldn't talk to me about the curse?" Best not to out Tait if I could help it.

"What does that have to do with pies?" He narrowed his eyes.

"That's not the important thing here. Why is the curse such a mystery? If you're worried I'll reveal some big se- cret, I'm not sure who you think I'll be talking to in Pilot Bay."

"It's not your problem," Leith said with a light growl to his tone.

"But maybe I could find a way to help, if you'd just tell me."

"How are you going to help? Are you a sorceress in disguise? Skilled in breaking blood curses?"

I opened my mouth to retort, but he didn't give me a chance to speak.

"You are only a girl, and you're stuck here and bored and see this great mystery. But it's not your problem, and it's not your business. Needing a diversion is not the same thing as caring."

Well, heck. That certainly stung. I brushed pastry crumbs off my silky mint skirt to hide the tears that threatened to fall. I couldn't think of what to say. Was he right? What could I do to fight magic?

Was I really only interested because I was bored? But then I thought of that blurred horizon creeping slowly inward, and of Ena and Deirdre and Tait, and even the surly beaver chefs.

I did care. Leith might be infuriating, but I certainly didn't want anything bad to happen to him.

While I scrambled to arrange my thoughts, Leith gathered himself to go.

"Stick to pies, *Àlainn*. You'll be back home soon enough."

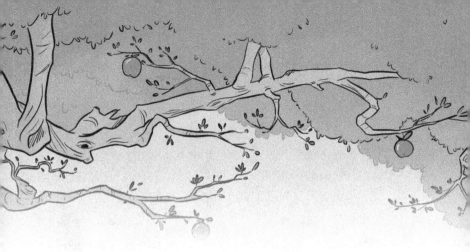

CHAPTER 13

"I DO CARE, YOU KNOW," I CALLED out over the hedge. The sound of boots on gravel paused as Leith stopped on the path. At least I assumed it was Leith, as no one else wore boots around here. Unless Tait had stolen some boots for his afternoon's mischief, which was possible, come to think of it.

"I'm not just bored." I sat up on my knees so I could see the path better from my favorite reading—and hiding—spot on the bench beside the fountain. It was indeed Leith. He had been tromping off somewhere with a sword on his back in his usual black casual daytime attire.

"I believe you," he replied gravely and then turned to continue on his way.

"I'm not bored *now*," I called after him, "but I'm going to become bored in about two more pages."

Leith turned back with raised eyebrows.

"I need a new book." I held up the nearly completed *Fenian Cycle* sadly.

"If you're this bad when you're entertained…"

"Hey!"

"Then I likely don't want to find out what you're like when you're idle."

I perked up. "I advise against it. Entertain me."

"Then, by all means, let's find you a new book."

Once inside, Leith led me through the castle to the back tower.

"Erm, aren't these your quarters?" I attempted to ask casually and instead managed to ask awkwardly.

"On the second level." He unlocked the door with a key from his belt. Thankfully, he didn't look back to catch my blush. "But I thought you'd like to see the library."

"Oh! I would." I followed Leith up a winding flight of stairs lit by candles that flickered into life ahead of us. I glanced back and watched as the flames sputtered out after we passed. More small magic. After a short climb, we paused on a landing, and the prince opened a pair of tall doors of golden carved wood that gleamed in the light of candles on either side.

"What do you think?" Leith asked as I walked past him into the room. But I was—for once—at a complete loss for words.

I don't know what I'd been expecting Kilinaire's library to be like, but nothing of this scale. The round tower room had to contain twice as many books as Pilot Bay's library. Shelves stretched from the carpeted floors up so high above that I'd be scared to stand on top of the rolling ladders of polished wood to reach the upper books.

The ceiling was painted a deep blue with strange constellations dotted across it in shining gold, and between the starry ceiling and the tops of the books, round windows let in the afternoon sun. In addition to the high windows, I counted three alcoves, each housing a tall stained-glass window. Two had study desks, and the third had a golden bowl on a tall wooden stand. The center of the library had a circle of comfortable seating and a glowing chandelier hanging above.

"The air feels different in here. Warmer?" I said absentmindedly as I walked to the books and ran my fingers reverently over gilded spines of linen and leather. Some were titled in English, some in what looked to be Irish, and many in characters I didn't even recognize.

"Magic." Leith leaned against the doorway, watching me explore the room. "My ancestor who built this tower designed the library as a gift for his lady. She was a scholar with a valuable collection of books. She was worried about bringing her books from the Seelie Court to a primitive rural manor like Kilinaire was at the time. The prince redesigned much of the castle to prove to her parents that he could provide a proper home for her, but this tower he built for her. There are strong spells of protection and preservation in the room to keep the books in perfect condition."

He walked over beside me and pulled a leather-bound book out from the shelf in front of me, his arm brushing my shoulder. I could feel his breath stir against my hair, and I held myself still until he stepped back, opening the book to show me a brightly illustrated page.

"See, the pages never yellow and the ink never fades. There isn't even any dust on the shelves."

"It's amazing. Are all these books from her collection?"

"No, maybe half of them. It still must have been quite a job to bring them here, even through the Rose Gate. The rest have been added over time. I'm not the first Prince of Kilinaire to enjoy reading."

"So many…" I turned slowly, taking them all in. "How many have you read?"

"All of them."

"Every one?"

"Nearly a hundred years with no outside company." He gently tucked the book back on the shelf. "I've had time."

It was the most he'd admitted about the curse, and I looked up at him, trying to imagine what that would be like. A hundred years without my sisters, Miss Chloe, or the little library kids. I liked my reading time, but I'm not sure I needed decades of it.

The sheer volume of books overwhelmed me. How could I possibly choose one out of thousands? There must be a system.

I was about to ask Leith to help me navigate when I again noticed the windowed alcove with an ornate golden bowl on a carved wooden stand. I walked over to examine it more closely. The bowl was held at waist height for one of the *Tuatha Dé Danann*, but more like chest height for a short human girl. It was filled to the brim with water. Even one more drop and it would spill over.

The stand holding the bowl was carved into the shape of curving thorny branches and delicate roses. It reminded me of the Rose Gate, as did the faint buzzing sensation I felt now that I was close to it. I stared into the bowl, expecting to see my reflection, but the water stayed dark. I could see the bottom of the golden bowl, but even when I stretched my hand over the water there was nothing reflected in it.

"What is it for?" I could feel Leith at my shoulder, watching me examine the bowl. I touched the side gingerly, feeling the buzz more strongly. "Is it solid gold?"

"It is solid gold, yes. Gold is one of the best materials for storing magic. It's why there are faerie gates in your forest. Your mountains were once rich with gold." Leith hovered his hand above the surface of the water. "Gold is rare in our world, but it's priceless for creating objects of power. A skilled crafter can create an object with a spell embedded in it so that anyone who knows how can use it. This one is a mirror."

"Did you make it?" I trailed a finger up the carving of a thorny vine.

"I don't have that kind of power, I'm afraid. It was created for my parents by Clíodhna, the Elder Fae who has watched over my kingdom since my ancestors ruled here, even before they joined the Seelie Kingdom. She's always been fond of roses."

"Impressive, but if it's a mirror, why doesn't it show any reflection?"

"It's not that kind of mirror. It allows me to see my lands and to communicate with other mirrors. A more powerful magic user can scry events from the past and even hints of the future."

"That still sounds handy," I said, watching the hair on the back of my arm stand up as I laid my hand on the side of the bowl.

"Less so since I've been cut off from my lands," Leith replied. "I can see the castle and a certain distance around the linked gate in the human world, but that's all."

"That's how you can tell what time of day it is in my forest and see the wolves."

"Yes."

"Can you still communicate with others? Is there someone out there who can help you with this curse, whatever it is? What about your ruler, the Seelie King? Surely he's powerful enough to help?"

"I can…I could communicate with another mirror." Leith hesitated. "Provided the person on the other side was able to scry for me at the right time, but as for the Seelie King, he clearly will not help me. If he even has the power to."

"Why not?" I glanced up, surprised. Leith's mouth was set in a hard line. "Aren't you under his protection? Isn't that how it works?"

"He will not help," Leith replied shortly. "Fiachra knows everything that happens in his realm. If he hasn't sent help in a hundred years, it can only mean that either he cannot break the curse, or he finds it convenient."

I wanted to push further, but I could tell by the look on his face that it wouldn't get me anywhere.

Leith sighed. "Here, let me show you how the mirror works. Magic is more about will than anything else. If you want to see something, you have to speak over the mirror, but you have to focus on the thing you wish to see, and you need to use the magic in the gold to activate it."

"Is that the buzzing feeling? The magic?"

"You can feel it?" Leith looked at me sharply.

"Should I not be able to?"

"I'm not sure. I didn't think you'd be able to, but I don't know much about how humans interact with the magic in our realm." Leith turned back to the bowl. He held his hand flat above the water, his long, scarred fingers outstretched as he muttered something. The water rippled as if a pebble had been dropped in it. I rose up on my tiptoes to see better, holding onto his sleeve for balance. The ripples cleared to show the path I had walked on to reach the faerie gate. I could see the stone cairn with the spirals on it, lit softly by the moonlight.

"It looks like a picture," I said, awestruck.

"Look there." Leith pointed to a moth above the cairn. It appeared still at first, but then its wings slowly unfurled as it flew. He spoke quietly, and the image shifted to the Rose Gate in my forest, the dark shadows of the wolves lurking through the trees. I shivered.

"This would be a really boring way to stalk someone," I whispered.

"Why are you whispering?" whispered Leith.

"I don't know," I whispered back.

I eyed the mirror with what I hoped was focus and will.

"Show me my sisters." I told the mirror. Nothing. Well, I guess it would have been too easy for me to just become magical during my stay here.

"Do I need to speak Irish for it to work?" I peered up at Leith. "Are you speaking Irish?"

"It's *Gaeilge Ársa*. The people of Ireland learned it from my people long ago, but it's changed there over time. And I don't know. I've never tried to teach a human magic.

The Elder Fae, Clíodhna would know, I'm sure, if we could only reach her."

"Well then, in the meantime…" I turned back to eye the library speculatively. "How about something to read."

"What did you have in mind?"

"No more death and glory," I told him. "Find me something with some romance in it."

CHAPTER 14

I FELL INTO A RHYTHM AS THE next week passed. A delicious breakfast in my room while chatting with Ena and Deirdre began each day, followed by some morning work, often with Tait. The little otter ignored further attempts of mine to pry information out of him. Sadly, Leith's threats must have finally sunk in. I even spent a couple of mornings gardening under the unsettling eye of Geanan. Lunch was served in the kitchen followed by an afternoon spent reading or exploring the grounds.

For dinner, Deirdre always produced a new dress in cool tones of water or leaves and bound my hair up with ribbons and gems. It seemed a bit much for a dinner with one other person, even if he was a prince, but dinner continued to be a formal affair. We'd eat roasted veggies and meat, discussing topics that ranged from the awkward to the inane, but he never let any more details slip about the curse. After dinner, I'd escape back to my rooms to enjoy an evening reading in front of the fire with Rani or soaking in the giant marble bath.

"What does he do all day?" I asked Tait as we ate lunch at the long table in the kitchen.

"Who?" Tait asked through a mouthful of pastry.

"The bear. Leith. I only ever seem to see him at dinner."

The clatter of the kitchen went suddenly silent.

"Why?" Tait popped another pastry into his mouth, and the beavers pretended to continue bustling about. But quietly.

"Um." It wasn't that odd of a question. Was it? "I'm almost done with my book," I said lamely, giving the book Leith had lent me from the library a tap. I mean, I was *almost*, almost done with my book.

"He trains after lunch. Back courtyard."

"Where?" I didn't remember coming across a back courtyard in my wanderings.

"I'll show you." Tait hopped off the bench in a fluid motion and disappeared out the back door.

"I didn't mean this second!" I said, grabbing the rest of my lunch and my book and running to catch up.

Tait ignored me and scampered along the gravel path following the castle wall before vanishing again around the corner.

"Obnoxious otter," I muttered. A door I'd previously overlooked on the castle wall was ajar. I stepped through and found it didn't lead inside as I had assumed but into a high-walled courtyard. On one wall, an awning shaded racks of weapons. Spears, bows, swords, and you know, other pointy objects. The rest of the space was a sandy open area with targets and posts—presumably to attack with pointy objects—scattered around it.

I must admit I only gave it all a quick glance, becoming immediately distracted by the sight of a shirtless Leith practicing some sort of complicated movement with a large sword. Shirtless.

Did I mention the lack of shirt? But there were a lot of lovely muscles. Apparently, he didn't spend all his time reading.

I tried to slide in without disturbing his concentration and nearly tripped over Tait and a pair of bunnies at my feet.

"Lot of cleaning needed in the courtyard this afternoon, then?" Tait asked the bunnies with a smirk.

"Oh sure," sighed the white bunny without taking her eyes off the prince.

"You never know when something might need dusting," agreed the spotted bunny with a matching sigh.

I eyed the bunnies with amusement, although I couldn't actually blame them for the sentiment.

"Why don't you ogle someone your own size?" Tait asked the bunnies grumpily.

"They don't make them like that in our size," replied the spotted bunny.

"I'm your size! Sort of. I could be if I had my powers back."

"Precisely my point." The spotted bunny wrinkled her nose at my friend.

Tait turned from the bunnies with a dignified huff. "Weren't you going to ask Lord Leith something?" he asked me.

"Was I?" I crouched down by the bunnies. "Where'd he get all those scars?" The bear prince's old injuries extended beyond his scarred hand and missing eye. Healed gashes started on his chest and covered his left shoulder and arm. They didn't seem to slow him down any, but the damage must have been terrible. I felt a twinge of guilt at the new scar on his right shoulder, still pink but fully healed. That must have been from our tangle with the wolves when I first arrived. Still, it looked pretty good for an injury from a week and a half ago. Must be magic.

"Ah, well, wolves, you know." The white bunny didn't take her eyes off the training prince.

"The same wolves that attacked me in the forest?"

The white bunny glanced up at me for the first time. "Aye, I'd say so."

131

"Stop telling her things," hissed Tait.

"It's fine. It's fine," I reassured the bunny. "What about the tattoo?"

"That would be from his time in the High Prince's fianna," she confided. "All Prince Tiernan's warriors are inked with his knot, you know."

"Interesting, interesting." I considered that tidbit for a moment. "But back to the wolves."

"Lord Leith doesn't like us talking about the curse!" Tait said in a whisper-yell. "Do you want me to get in further trouble?"

"Not everything," sniffed the spotted bunny, "is about you." And with that the two bunnies hopped off.

"I'd better go, too," I whispered to Tait. "He looks busy. I'll catch him at dinner like usual." I didn't have a lot of moral high ground over the ogling bunnies, and I was pretty sure this situation would be a whole lot less awkward if I just snuck out without being noticed.

Tait rolled his eyes and muttered something about ridiculous females while I tiptoed out of the courtyard.

"*Àlainn*," Leith called from behind me.

I froze in the doorway.

"How do you feel about bees?"

I turned, confused. He had apparently finished training for the day as he'd pulled his shirt on. Which was good. But sad.

"Bees? They are…rather stripy?" I answered. "Why?"

"I need to get the hives ready for winter. Would you be willing to help? It's a job easiest done if the second set of hands is, in fact, hands and not paws."

"Oh, um, okay?" I said nervously. "I've never worked with bees before though."

"Ena will get you suited up with netting and some thick gloves. Nothing to worry about."

I nodded and stepped out of the courtyard. Was it the thought of the bees that was tying my insides in knots or the beekeeper?

CHAPTER 15

I MET LEITH OUTSIDE A LITTLE WHILE later at the edge of the orchard where I had picked apples with Tait. I was equipped with a sturdy long-sleeved dress, boots, gloves, and a wide-brimmed straw hat with a veil of netting on it. Leith was in boots and thick woolen pants, but he was bare-headed, and the arms of his linen shirt were rolled up, the scars on the back of his left forearm disappearing into his sleeve. More comfortable under the warm autumn sun, perhaps, but short sleeves struck me as completely reckless.

"Aren't you worried about being stung?" I asked him in horror.

"Oh, the bees don't usually bother me." He shrugged. "And there are worse things in life than being stung."

"Probably true, but I'd still prefer to avoid it." I flipped my veil down and fiddled with the edge. I was so focused on not panicking about swarms of bees that I didn't notice Leith moving until I felt his hands gently pushing mine away from the edge of the veil. He tightened the tie that kept the netting drawn in enough at the bottom to discourage buzzing intruders and adjusted the drape of the veil.

I looked up at him and watched the brush of his good eye's tawny eyelashes across his cheek as he finished getting me ready. His eye patch had been ever-present on the other eye since that first day. Was it comfortable, or did it annoy him? Did he wear it just to keep from upsetting me with his scarred appearance? His gray eye flicked to mine briefly, but he turned away before I could read the expression in it.

"This way," he said, walking over to a row of straw baskets that emitted a buzzing hum. The baskets were shaped like the beehives from children's books, and the row of five baskets stood on a low wooden bench. Bees crawled in and out of the hole each basket had near the bottom, and they flew thickly in the air. I took a deep breath and followed him, trying not to flinch as a stray bee bounced off my veil before flying off.

"So, what are we doing with the bees, exactly?" My question came out with more of a squeak than I intended as he smoothly flipped a basket over.

"We're collecting the honey today. Then I need to get the remaining hives ready for the cold, so I can move them to the rose garden later to overwinter."

"Why the rose garden? Is there less snow? And shouldn't you spray those baskets with smoke or something first?" I peeked around his shoulder. Masses of bees crawled over rows of honeycomb inside. "I watched a documentary once. There was smoke."

"The rose garden…" He paused. Possibly trying to decide what to tell me. Maybe trying to guess what a documentary was. "It's a safer spot for them this year." He moved on briskly, "The baskets are called skeps. They're the hives. And the bees don't really like smoke. Don't worry." He said something low and musical to the bees in the skep, and their busy industry slowed to a lethargic hum. Leith held out the basket to me, a bee crawling idly over his knuckles, and I took the basket in my arms automatically, before I could think better of it.

I stood there holding the skep mutely, staring at the golden honeycomb crawling with bees. Now what?

Leith flipped over the next hive, talking to it in the same musical tone. He must have been magically calming the bees. Then he set it upside down on the ground against his legs and motioned me over. With his direction, I clumsily set my skep over his, with their open ends together. And then to my surprise he started hitting the top hive.

"Um, won't that make them angry?" I took a nervous step back.

"The bottom skep is a good one to overwinter in," explained Leith, drumming away on the basket. "I'm convincing the bees in the top skep to move in. Then we can harvest the honey out of the empty hive."

He tipped the top basket up slightly, and I saw the bees pouring down into the bottom hive.

"Oh!" I'd never seen anything like that, and I came closer to see, forgetting to be worried.

After two more smacks to the top skep, Leith flipped it over and examined the remaining bees. With another magical word, a large bee crawled onto his outstretched finger.

"Is that the queen?" I asked, awestruck.

Leith nodded and coaxed the bee into the bottom hive. Another few drums and he handed me the top hive, deftly covering the one he still had with a cloth before carefully turning it over and replacing it on the wooden bench.

We did the same with the rest of the hives on the bench, stacking three empty hives in a wagon, and then Leith whispered something as he ran his hand across the two bee-filled skeps he had declared good for winter.

"What did you say to them?" I asked as we walked across the orchard to the castle, Leith pulling the wagon behind us.

"It's a small magic." He parked the wagon and we started unloading the hives onto the kitchen steps. "It keeps the hive healthy. Seals it from predators and diseases."

More of this *small magic*. I fingered the hair ribbon Deirdre had spelled this morning for me.

Leith rapped on the kitchen door, and a beaver poked its head out and came to haul the honey-filled skeps into the kitchen.

"What counts as small magic?"

"Hmm, most things. It's hard to think of it all. Keeping things warm, preservation from dust and rot, small healings."

"Like my ankle?" It hadn't held my weight in the forest, but I'd run on it after waking.

"Yes, I healed your ankle while you slept."

"Thank you."

He nodded and headed back into the orchard, toward another row of hives. I followed, half jogging to keep up.

"What about putting me to sleep when you first brought me here? That was small magic?"

"That too," he admitted.

"Don't do it again," I grumbled, remembering the feeling of being put to sleep like a child while intentionally forgetting the feeling of being swept up in strong arms.

"Next time, I'll let the wolves eat you then," he replied, a hint of teasing in his voice.

"Thank you," I said primly.

We worked in comfortable silence for a while. I felt like I was getting the hang of it as we stacked three more skeps on the kitchen steps, although I was clearly no competition for Leith with his experience and small magics.

"Beekeeping doesn't seem like something a…what exactly are you? A prince, would do?"

"Yes, a Seelie prince, technically, although I'm not prince of much anymore," he answered, closing up the hive.

"Right, you mentioned the Seelie Court. Seelies are the good faeries, right? And Unseelies are bad?" I asked, thinking I should search the library for more information on types of faeries.

"Not exactly. The Seelie Fae are more civilized. We form stronger bonds and tend to live in community. Our domain is in the south of Tír na nÓg where the climate is milder for farming. Seelie Fae like order and stability above all else. This can be good, but it can also be…"

"Boring?" I supplied.

"Well, that, yes. Sometimes. But I was going to say Seelie Fae don't adapt well to change. Now, Unseelie Fae tend to live more solitary lives, each looking out for themselves. The Unseelie Queen has a court, and there are small family groups, but by and large, they live alone. They often embrace chaos and can be destructive, but they are not, as a whole, evil. And the Seelie are not, as a whole, good. Each faerie makes its own choices in the world."

"Just as humans do," I said.

He led me to the next row of hives. "The beekeeping is not traditionally a prince's job, no. I've picked it up since…"

"The curse," I put in helpfully.

"The curse," he agreed. "It's an easier job for someone with hands to manage. And easier with two pairs of them today. Thank you."

"No problem." I attempted to blithely ignore the swarm of bees covering the skep he was handling. "So, if you're a prince, are you supposed to be a king someday?"

"No, I'm not that sort of prince. Kilinaire is all that's left of the Rose Court, a princedom under the Seelie King. We manage the land between the northern border and the southern plains. It's mostly forested, but there's the castle, the village across the river, and a fair bit of farmland." He handed me a frame, and I stacked it in the wagon. "It's nothing very exciting."

"It sounds wonderful." I tried to imagine what a childhood here would have been like. "I grew up in a big city, and it's never quiet there. Not really. I didn't realize how much it was always wearing on me until we moved to Pilot Bay and our house on the edge of the forest. My sister Amber complains about living in the middle of nowhere, but it doesn't feel like that to me. It feels like enough space to finally breathe."

"I know what you mean," Leith said. "When I spent time at the court as a child, I was always escaping to the forest with Tiernan as soon as I could. The Seelie Court is beautiful, without a doubt, but I like the peace of the woods. Even Kilinaire felt like too much at times." He paused, watching the bees hum above us in the apple tree. "I never thought I'd be tired of being by myself, but the past hundred years have proved me wrong."

"But you have Ena, and Tait, and the other faeries still? I mean, I know it's probably not the same as your family, but you're not really alone, are you?" I said hesitantly. Maybe it was some sort of prince/servant thing, although Ena didn't seem like the type to stand on ceremony.

"I would be, quite literally, lost without Ena," agreed Leith. "But I'm the one who brought this curse on us all, that caused the loss of so many of their loved ones. I'll never be one of them."

"So, they're not allowed to forgive you, then?"

He was silent as we loaded the last of the hives into the wagon. I'd almost given up on him answering as we walked back toward the castle, but at last he spoke softly.

"Some things aren't forgivable. I've done my best to be a good prince in the time since, to take care of those who remain, but it's a drop in the bucket compared to what I've done. There's no atoning for it."

For what?! I railed internally, but as chatty as he was today, I didn't think he'd tell me. And that wasn't really the point here.

"Not forgivable by them? I'm not sure I agree, but what about by God? Is he allowed to forgive you?"

Leith walked beside me in silence again. Maybe I'd pushed him too far.

"Or whatever you believe in?" I asked. Did the fae have religions?

"If God is just and wise, then he will not forgive me either," said Leith.

And what about you? I thought. *Will you ever forgive yourself?* But I didn't say the words out loud. I already knew the answer.

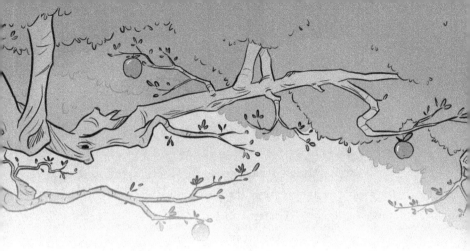

CHAPTER 16

IT HAD BEEN TWELVE DAYS SINCE I had come to Kilinaire, and I was frustrated that I still hadn't solved the mystery of the curse. I had spent the morning with Tait, harvesting carrots under the watchful eye of Geanan. Tait had been unable to resist playing a trick on Geanan—something involving a pitchfork and a pile of auroch manure—and I was on my own for lunch while he wisely hid in the back pond.

Without his chatty company, I opted for my book and a bench in the hedge maze across from the faerie lady's fountain. It was already further into autumn than when I had arrived, but the roses remained exuberant and their scent filled the air around me.

I was finishing my apple when a shadow crossed over my book.

"Are you enjoying the story?" Leith sat as I scooted over to make room for him on the carved stone bench.

"I am, although I have to say, it doesn't strike me as the sort of thing you would recommend." I flipped to the embossed cover. "Tristan and Iseult?"

"I can't enjoy a good romance?" he asked me, a tug of a smile on his lips. I'd yet to get a full smile out of him. I'd have to try harder. I tapped the book and eyed him skeptically.

"It was my sister's book," he admitted. "Her favorite, so I thought you might like it."

So much for making him smile.

"I do like it."

No response from the fae prince who was watching the fountain. Super chatty, this guy. "Are you ever going to tell me about her? Neala?"

"Are you ever going to tell me your name?" he asked in return, still using his standard deflection.

"You promise you won't use it to turn me into a mindless drone?"

"I swear it." He gave a hint of that smile. "That's not how magic works."

"Hmmm..." I drew the moment out, even though I'd long since stopped being afraid of anything the bear might do. I wasn't sure why I hadn't told him yet. Maybe I didn't mind being someone else for a while. Isobel was quiet, anxious, and ran away from her problems. I wasn't always sure I liked her. *Àlainn* seemed to be better at standing up for herself. How could I bring *Àlainn* home with me when I left the castle?

"Story first." I turned to face him on the bench and crossed my legs up under my dress. He narrowed his eyes, but I could tell something had shifted between us, and not just on my side. Maybe he was slowly learning to trust me as well.

"You drive a hard bargain, *Àlainn*."

I just smiled expectantly.

He sighed and settled back against the bench, gazing back at the fountain. I held my breath, waiting to see if he would actually tell me this time instead of coming up with more, increasingly flimsy, excuses.

And then, finally, he began.

"Neala was my younger sister. I grew up with her tagging along after me through the castle grounds. Kilinaire was a wonderful place to grow up, just wild enough to have adventures. We spent a few weeks of the year at court, but for the most part Neala and I only had each other as playmates.

"When I was old enough, I began service in one of the Seelie King's war bands, his Fianna, as all noble fae sons are required to do. I trained with his heir, Prince Tiernan, and later was part of his smaller fianna, patrolling the border between the Seelie and Unseelie kingdoms. I came home for a few weeks a year, but I didn't see much of my family during those years. It was expected I would return home after a few decades with the Fianna and learn the running of the Rose Court from my father. But that wasn't what happened. I had only been away from Kilinaire for a handful of years when I received news that my parents had died. They had been visiting the Seelie Court and were killed in a hunting accident."

"Both of them?"

"It seemed suspicious to me as well, especially as my mother didn't have a great love for hunting, but I talked to witnesses. Apparently, they had gone on a hunt for a wyvern, and my mother stumbled too close to its lair and hidden kits. My father tried to save her, but both of them were killed before the rest of the party was able to defeat the beast."

I covered my mouth. "Oh, Leith."

"King Fiachra told me personally. He offered me the head of the wyvern, but I couldn't stand the sight of it. I believe he had it mounted and hung in his throne room." Leith's tone was acidic.

"And so, you became the prince."

"I did. I was very young to become Prince, and I had avoided learning as much as I should have about my duties from my parents. I thought I still had centuries before I would have to take up that responsibility. I struggled. I am not naturally good at winning people's loyalty, and my heart wasn't in the task. I was sure my parents' deaths hadn't been a simple accident. I heard rumors that they had been speaking out in court, opposing King Fiachra's policies involving the treatment of the *aes sídhe*, the small fae, by the Seelie nobility.

"I was obsessed with finding answers. Keeping track of the harvest and settling disputes between villagers seemed of little consequence in comparison. I could see the kingdom was slipping under my rule, although Neala was much better at managing it than I was. She had a gift for understanding people and making them feel heard. Knowing the details of our people's lives gave her a sense of purpose and belonging. But, to me, it was suffocating.

"One day, needing a break, I went hunting with no one but my horse in the mountains at the edge of our lands. The Unseelie Queen was waiting for me there, in the empty wilderness, as if she knew I would be there. Which, I suppose she must have."

"Is she beautiful?" Not that it mattered to me if he was in the habit of meeting beautiful fae ladies in the woods.

"Queen Moriath is…yes. She is beautiful. She is beautiful and wild and savage, with hair like flowing ice and eyes that are barely warmer. Before that time, I had only seen her from afar in border skirmishes with the Unseelie Fianna. I had heard it said that she was known to collect young men the way some women collect cats, but when she spoke to me it was as if we were the only two people who existed."

I pretty much hated this Unseelie Queen already.

"She asked me to join her court," he said at last. "She promised me a life of privilege without responsibility, but more than that, she dropped hints that she knew the truth of what had happened to my parents. I wish I could say it was only a need for justice that drove me, but I knew I was failing as a prince. Rather than trying to humble myself to learn, I was given the opportunity to leave it all behind. To run away. And I agreed."

I held my breath now, not wanting to break the spell of his story.

"While I had found brothers in my time with the Fianna, that life was taken from me, and I never felt at home among the general Seelie Fae. The bonds of community and friendship seemed to slide off me, and without my parents, there was only Neala left. I told myself she would be better off if I left. She was a natural leader, and our people loved her, small fae and high fae alike. I would do more good elsewhere.

"I swore a blood oath to the Unseelie Queen." He held out his right hand to me, palm up, and I took it in mine to examine it better. His left arm and hand bore the obvious scars, but now I saw he also had a red scar running across his right palm. Without thinking, I began to trace it with my finger, but Leith balled his hand up and pulled away again.

"But still my heart held something back." Leith clenched his scarred hand. "I told her I needed to say goodbye to Neala. I had to explain myself to my sister.

What would she think if I just disappeared? The queen didn't want to let me go. I think she knows her influence is strongest when she's with someone, but she agreed in the end. She gave me one week to say goodbye before making my way to her palace in the north. She reminded me again of all the reasons I wished to bind myself to her, hinted again that she had knowledge of my parents' deaths, and she sent a falcon with me, a kestrel."

"What for?"

"The fae monarchs have the ability to use birds as messengers. The Seelie King uses ravens, and the Unseelie Queen, falcons. The bird was meant to keep an eye on me, although she merely said he was a way to send word to her if I had any trouble on my journey to her court. Before I left, she kissed my forehead and her lips felt like ice. Ice so cold it felt like fire against my skin. It spread through my veins and filled me with a clarity I badly wanted. One week, and then I would be hers."

CHAPTER 17

BUT YOU AREN'T, ARE YOU?" I felt a shiver run down my spine. I pushed his hair back from his forehead, but I didn't see any mark on it.

"No, *Àlainn*, I'm not." He looked into my eyes for the first time since he'd begun telling his story. "Not yet, anyway. But don't skip ahead."

I dropped my hand and looked away, my cheeks heating.

"When I got back home, Neala was, of course, upset. It was more than my announcement that I was leaving. She later said there was a coldness in my eyes that terrified her. She begged and pleaded with me to stay, but I packed a few belongings and signed over the estate to her. Finally, she relented, or at least she told me that she had. She told me she understood that I needed to go, but begged me to wait one more night. If I would only stay until morning, she would send me with her blessing. Normally I would have seen through her lie with ease, but with the queen's kiss still burning in me, my purpose was so clear that it only made sense she would agree to it.

"The next morning, she walked me to the Rose Gate and kissed me goodbye. She kissed me on the forehead right over the queen's invisible mark and whispered, 'Be free.' I felt the warmth of her kiss chase the icy magic out of my mind, and with tears in her eyes, my beloved sister again begged me to stay. And this time I agreed.

"She later told me she had left during the night to seek the help of Clíodhna, the Elder Fae. Clíodhna told my sister how to break the queen's magic if she had enough love and strength of will to do so.

"I agreed to stay, but the cut on my hand burned cold, and I worried it might not be so simple. I told Neala of my foolish oath, but she was sure that with the breaking of the compulsion spell, I was free."

"What about the falcon?" I asked.

"It was gone, which made me all the more troubled. But my week ran out, and nothing happened. Moriath didn't swoop down and carry me off. The countryside remained peaceful. Week after week passed and still nothing. Gradually I began to relax. I allowed Neala to infect me with her optimism. I should have been more vigilant."

I could hear the despair in his voice, and my fingers itched to reach over and take his hand again, but I held them tightly in my lap as he continued.

"One day." He took a breath and seemed to will himself to continue. "One day in the early autumn, I was hunting. I returned home late in the afternoon, and Neala wasn't there. The household fae told me she had gone to the village to take some food to a needy family there. A perfectly ordinary explanation, but I still felt a sense of unease. As the afternoon wore on, my unease grew, and as the sun began to set, I paced the front garden path, waiting. I had just made up my mind to saddle my horse and follow after her when an ancient fae walked up to the Rose Gate and called out to me.

"She had the appearance of a tree faerie, so wrinkled with age that her brown skin had the knots and whorls of an old oak tree.

"'Prince,' she called out, 'I have walked far and am tired. Please, may I stay the night?'

"Now, as you know, the Rose Gate is the only way into the castle grounds, and it's spelled to keep intruders out."

I nodded. That must be why I'd walked under the roses to the meadow twice without coming through the gate to Kilinaire.

"Only Neala or I could let someone new through the gate, and it takes a great deal of will to do so. Not only was I unwilling to postpone leaving long enough to allow her entry, I admit I was so nervous about the Unseelie

Queen's revenge that I trusted no stranger. I didn't want her staying in the castle without me there, and I needed to go check on Neala. So, I suggested she make her way across the bridge to the village. I tossed her a coin through the gate to get a room at the village inn and turned to go collect my horse.

"She protested that she was too tired to walk to the village, but I turned a deaf ear and began to walk away.

"'But sir,' she begged one last time, 'The light is nearly gone and there are wolves in these woods.'

"I turned back to her, now sure I was being tricked for I knew these woods better than anyone. 'Begone,' I told her with a wave of my hand, 'there has never been a wolf in these woods.'

"But I was wrong.

"As I turned the bend in the path to head to the stable, I heard them. A sound you are all too familiar with now as well. The howling of a pack of wolves on the hunt.

"I spun and ran back to the gate to let her in, but I was too late. And as the wolves descended on her, the ancient faerie melted away, and my own dear sister was revealed in her place. She had been disguised, a spell of compulsion binding her. I managed to fight the wolves off, even un-armed as I was... But I was too late for Neala." He paused and rubbed the scars on his arm.

"That's what happened to your eye." It was not quite a question.

"My eye is nothing." Leith turned and faced me at last, and I could see how fresh his pain still was, even after a hundred years. "I would have died for her. I should have died for her.

"If I had let the old lady in. If I had kept my promise to the queen. If I had not made that blood oath. If I had-...just been a better ruler, a more dutiful son, a more thoughtful brother. She would still be alive. I was given so many chances to save her, and I wasted every one of them."

He held himself so stiffly, the inches between us felt like miles. What could I say to that?

"I'm so sorry," I managed, knowing it didn't change anything.

He kept going as if I hadn't spoken.

"When darkness fell fully, she came. Riding on a reindeer through the woods, glowing like an angel. She knelt down in front of me as I held my sister's body on the ground and cupped my ruined cheek with her cold hand. 'Now will you come to me?' Moriath asked. And if I hadn't known already, I understood then that she had arranged this whole game as a punishment for me. For daring to choose my sister over her.

"And still she thought I might come to her freely. She understands so little of love. I snarled wordlessly at her and sprang to attack, but she simply said, 'If you wish to act like a beast, you may be one. But one way or another, you will be mine.' And I fell to the ground, unconscious.

"When I woke, I was alone in the forest, in the shape of a bear. I soon realized I wasn't even in Faerie anymore, but in your forest, in the human world. I wandered as a bear for countless days before a raccoon found me and led me back through the Rose Gate."

"Ena?" I guessed. He nodded.

"Yes, Ena brought me back to the castle. A refuge from the curse even though you can feel the dark magic fueled from my broken oath and Neala's death pressing in on it."

I shivered. It must have been her dying screams I'd heard when I had touched the edge of the protective bubble.

"We found more of the household," Leith went on, "and brought them to the castle where, even if they remained in animal form, at least they had their speech back."

"You can't speak when you're in the human world?" I asked.

"No, and many of the household never found their way home. I don't know what happened to them, but I would guess wild animals found them in the forest, or they slowly became wild themselves.

"There was more land surrounding the castle then, and I did my best to keep everyone fed and safe. A responsibility I should have taken on from the start. I don't know why the castle has been safe all these years. I can only guess that there is a powerful counterspell at work.

But it erodes a little more every night, and someday our time will be up."

"And then what?"

"And then the Unseelie Queen wins, I suppose. With my prison gone, I will be hers. Maybe I can bargain at the end and see if she'll transform Ena, Tait, and the others back to their faerie forms. I owe them much more than that."

I was struck again by the despair in his voice. "But isn't there anything…"

"No, *Àlainn*, there's nothing," he said harshly, rising to leave. "My punishment has been delayed, but it is justly earned. And now that you know my story—what sort of man I truly am—I will understand if you wish to have dinner in your room tonight."

I watched him as he disappeared back into the hedge maze. I doubted he had any idea of the sort of man he truly was. I stayed by the fountain for a while, my book forgotten on my lap, with tears running down my cheeks for the proud young prince and the sister who had loved him above all else.

CHAPTER 18

INSTEAD OF COMING WITH A NEW DRESS for me in blues or purples for the evening, Deirdre and Ena instead came with a basket full of piping hot food from the kitchen for dinner.

"He was serious then." I felt more than a bit grumpy, even though the food smelled amazing.

"He was," confirmed Ena. I was unsurprised that she knew what I was talking about. There wasn't much in the castle that was secret from Ena.

"Maybe I'll have a bath then," I said halfheartedly, plucking a meat pastry out of the basket.

"Okay, miss!" Deirdre scampered off to the bathroom.

"I can do it," I called after her, but she was already out of sight. A moment later I heard the water running.

"You have to understand, my dear, he's a very private man. Opening himself up to you like that…it wasn't a small thing."

"So now he's shutting himself up again?" I took a vicious bite of pastry. Was that pork? It was really good. But that was beside the point. "Where can I find him tomorrow? Surely he won't want to eat in his rooms again?"

"Actually…" Ena started hesitantly.

"What is it, Ena?"

"You're going home tomorrow." My stomach dropped like a rock as she continued. "The prince says morning is breaking in the human world, and the wolves will be leaving soon. You'll be safe to use the Rose Gate."

That's why Leith had finally opened up to me. He knew I was leaving anyway.

Ena didn't seem any happier about the news than I felt. I supposed I should be excited to go home to my sisters and my life in Pilot Bay, but things felt unfinished here.

"Your bath is ready," announced Deirdre, popping back into the room.

"Thank you." I tried not to think about how I would miss the little fox. Hopefully I'd get a chance to find Tait in the morning before I left.

And so, I spent my last night in the castle with only my thoughts for company. I stayed in the bath longer than I should have to finish my book so I could return it to Leith in the morning. Eventually, I pulled my pruned self out and went to bed. I slept restlessly with dreams of wolves and icy fae queens.

The next morning Deirdre and Ena appeared with my breakfast and the torn, yellow jersey dress I'd been wearing when I arrived.

"It is, of course, up to you, my dear." Ena opened my curtains and let in the early morning light. It was overcast this morning, which rather suited my mood. "You can tell your family the truth, if you think they'll believe you. But it may be wiser to slip back into your old life and carry on as if nothing happened."

It seemed impossible to me to forget about my time here, to act as though these past two weeks hadn't ever happened, but I understood the wisdom in not showing up at the cabin in a faerie gown with pearls in my hair and unbelievable stories. So, after breakfast, I pulled on my muddy dress and sat in front of the mirror. Deirdre did my hair, like every other morning in the castle, but this time she carefully tangled and muddied my hair, adding twigs and dead leaves with the same eye to detail as she would have with gems and ribbons. Ena produced a jar of mud, and I laughed, despite my somber mood, as we painted it on.

"Did I really look this ragged when I got here?" I asked my furry friends.

"Worse," confirmed Ena. "But you probably don't want to reinjure your ankle for authenticity's sake."

"Yeah, I'm good with just the twigs and mud." I winced at the memory. "Thank you, Ena, for making me feel so at home here." I knelt down and hugged the raccoon. "I hope you're able to get back to your faerie forms someday."

"Oh, don't you worry about us now." Ena's tone was brisk, but her eyes glinted with tears.

I scooped up Deirdre, and the little fox made a surprised squeak, but she laid her snout on my shoulder as I gave her a hug. "Thank you for taking such good care of me," I said. "I'm sure I've never looked so beautiful as I have with your help."

"I only wish we had managed to sew you up a proper gown, my lady, but I suppose we didn't have an occasion to truly warrant one."

"Well, you made me feel like a princess." I set her down again.

A loud knock on the door made us all jump. "It's time to go," said a rough voice through the door.

"The charm never ceases with that one." Ena rolled her eyes. "But, you'd best be off."

I paused with my hand on the doorknob. "You'll say goodbye to Tait and the others for me?" Ena nodded, and on a whim, I stepped back and knelt in front of her, asking under my breath, "What is it that he keeps calling me? *Àlainn*?"

Ena gave a surprised bark of laughter, covering her mouth with her paw.

"What?" Had Leith been poking fun at me for the past two weeks? It probably meant "scruffy human" or "talks too much."

"It means 'beauty,' my dear," she said softly, patting my hand. "And he's not wrong about that."

This whole time he had been calling me *Beauty*? Well, that made me feel a bit flustered.

I stood up and looked one more time around the lovely blue room that had been my home in the castle before opening the door.

Leith stood there, impassively watching me with his steely gray eye. His dark hair was still tied back neatly, and I thought of how frightened I'd been of him when I'd arrived. Not that he was being exactly warm and fuzzy right now, but I wasn't fooled.

"It's a good look for me, eh?" I touched my hair, hoping to coax that half smile out of him. He leaned forward, like he was on the edge of saying something, but instead he silently turned and strode off down the hall, leaving me running to catch up with his long legs.

Outside it was drizzling lightly, but Leith didn't seem to notice. I glanced at him sidelong as we walked down the stone path to the Rose Gate, but he didn't betray his thoughts. Maybe he was happy to have his peace and quiet back, no matter what he'd said while we harvested honey.

When we stopped in front of the Rose Gate, he turned to me at last.

"The wolves are gone, and the mirror showed your family out looking for you. You should find them if you keep to the path."

"Those aren't normal wolves." It wasn't quite a question.

"No, they are young men the Unseelie Queen has tired of, still bound to her will."

"Why does she care who wanders in the forest at night?"

"I suppose she doesn't want to risk anything upsetting her spell further. She can't be happy that she's had to wait to claim me, but she's willing to be patient."

I had a hundred questions, still, about the curse. What could she be worrying about upsetting it? Leith said there was no hope of breaking the spell, but if that were true, why bother with the wolves? I stared through the Rose Gate, at the path through the woods of Faerie that I would never travel, and I knew I was stalling. My adventure was over, my family was looking for me, and clearly the prince, for all his cryptically flattering nicknames, was not overly bothered by my leaving.

"Well, then," I took a breath and turned to face Leith. "Thank you for everything. Goodbye, Bear."

I turned away and took a step, only to be stopped as my hand was caught from behind. I stared at my small hand wrapped in his long, scarred fingers. My breath caught, but all he said was, "Goodbye, *Àlainn*."

"Isobel," I whispered and looked up to catch his gaze. "My name is Isobel."

And then I took another step back, my hand slipping out of his, and the castle and its prince disappeared as I stepped through the Rose Gate and back into my forest.

PART
3

CHAPTER 19

I STAYED FOR A MINUTE AT THE edge of the clearing the miner's cabin still stood in, staring at the Rose Gate. The mist had disappeared with the castle, and I was standing barefoot in the dew as the sun rose over the mountains.

I felt numb, but I gave myself a mental shake and found the path that led home.

When Leith said my family was looking for me, I'd imagined a teary Lily calling for me through the woods, or maybe my dad, but it was Amber who found me at the crossroads of the ATV trail.

"Bel!" She flung her arms around me, nearly cutting off my air with the force of her hug. "Oh, Isobel, I'm so sorry for being such a brat at supper. What were you thinking? Running off in the dark?! Just tell me to shut up next time."

"Are you crying?" I asked her as soon as I could breathe again.

"What? No! Shut up!" She pulled back and wiped her eyes with her hand. "What happened to you? You look awful. More than usual, I mean."

There was the sister I knew. Just then, a frantic Lily and my father, looking rather more haggard than usual, came running up the trail. Lily fussed over me, and Dad seemed relieved to find me alive. Apparently, they had found my missing sandals and bag rather worse for the wear, thanks to the wolves, and had feared they wouldn't find me at all, alive or otherwise.

I felt a bit guilty for spending what had essentially been a fairy tale vacation in a castle while they had been searching for me, but I reminded myself that it had only been one night of worry for them, and that I hadn't had much of a choice. I was grateful the wolves had been too focused on me to terrorize my family. Even Amber.

As we headed down the mountain trail back to our house, I told them the short—by which I mean believable—version of my story. That I'd been chased briefly by wolves, then escaped when a bear decided to take them on. Too scared to go past them back to the house, I'd hidden in the miner's cabin and fallen asleep.

"I'm really sorry you guys were so worried," I finished lamely. "I would have come home, but I was so tired from running, and I must have drifted off." It sounded unbelievable even to me, but after all, what else could I have been doing in the forest all night? What had really happened was far stranger.

When we got home, I had a hot bath, and Lily brought me tea and cookies.

"Are you sure you're alright?" Lily settled down on the floor beside the tub. Gone were my private baths at Kilinaire. No modesty between sisters, after all. "You're not just in shock or something?"

She'd already called Miss Chloe and told her I wouldn't be in at the library today. I would have been happy to get back to work, but I agreed anyway because Lily was right. I should be traumatized by a night in the forest being chased by wolves. And I had been, two weeks ago.

"I'm okay."

And it was almost true. It was strange being back home. It felt like a dream, and I would wake up and be back at Kilinaire.

"I'm sorry for running off like that. Causing so much trouble just to avoid listening to them argue. I shouldn't let it get to me like I do."

Lily sighed and stole a cookie off the plate. "It's hard for me, too," she said around a mouthful of snickerdoodle. "I sometimes feel like if I could think of the right thing to say, if I could just make the perfect meal, we could have peace in this house. But Amber's so…"

"Obnoxious?" I suggested. Although, she'd hugged me so tightly in the forest this morning. Sniping aside, we were still sisters.

"Angry."

"And Dad barely talks, unless she manages to bait him into fighting with her."

"Maybe that's why she does it," mused Lily.

"Are you ever angry, Lil?" She was always so calm, even after all she'd been forced to give up in the past year. I almost felt bad about how much I loved living in Pilot Bay. It seemed like punishment for the rest of my family.

"I was angry at first, for sure," she said agreeably. "But I'll find my way back to school. And as for the money, I guess it was never really mine to start with. But you?" She tucked a stray hair behind my ear. "You're mine. You and Amber both. Another couple of years with you guys until you're out the door and into the world? It's a gift, even if it's not what I would have chosen."

I tried to answer, but my throat was closed with tears, so I just rested my head against hers and was at last grateful to be back home.

I did my best to slip back into my everyday life. The real world, I guess, although it didn't feel as real as life at Kilinaire Castle. I took the rest of the week off work at Lily's insistence, and to be honest, I didn't mind the time to adjust to being home. I went to the beach with Amber and helped Lily in the kitchen. I sat on the back porch with my book in the evenings, listening to the trees stir in the breeze, not ready to go for a hike that didn't lead back to that little corner of Tír na nÓg. The forest for its own sake had lost its pull on me.

Amber snapped at me less for the first few days, chattering around me in her own attempt to cheer me up. Lily made all my favorite meals. Dad still worked and drank, and occasionally I caught him watching me in a way that seemed vaguely guilty although I couldn't imagine what for. Maybe for fighting with Amber. For not being a watchful parent. But I could be imagining things. It's not like I knew him that well.

The next Monday, I went back to my story-reading and glitter-wrangling at the library. When I hugged the last class of kids goodbye, Miss Chloe found me flipping through the book I'd been reading to the children. It was a collection of old fairy tales from Germany, many of which were gruesome in a way that terrified the girls and thrilled the boys.

"What story was it today? *The Singing Bone?*" She peeked at the book over my shoulder.

I laughed. "Nothing so horrifying as that. We did *Hansel and Gretel*. It was bad enough. Full of abandoned children and cannibal witches. Hopefully we don't get phone calls from angry parents whose kids woke up screaming in the night."

Miss Chloe settled into the chair next to mine. "That was always the purpose of those tales, especially the German ones. A little fear to remind you to listen to your elders."

"Or end up on the brunch menu for a witch?"

"That's what happens to sassy children!" she agreed lightly. "Next week you start Norse Mythology, right?"

"Yes, by Odin," I confirmed. "You should know. You put the program together."

"I always liked the Norse tales," Miss Chloe said thoughtfully. "Especially since that nice Chris Hemsworth started playing Thor."

I let out a surprised laugh. "Miss Chloe! You're clearly a stickler for authenticity," I teased.

"Those biceps looked plenty authentic to me," sighed Miss Chloe happily. "So how is it, being back?"

I froze, then forced myself to relax. Of course, she meant back at work after my *traumatic experience* and subsequent time off. Not back in the human world.

"Oh, it's fine," I assured her. "I'm fine."

She got up and started clearing the craft table. "Have you been back in the forest since that night? Solved the mystery of the shifty roses?"

I stacked chairs around her. "No, I'm just..." I paused, holding a chair, "I don't feel like I should take off hiking anymore. Everyone expects me to be afraid of the forest now." Lily, especially, watched me like a hawk every time I left the house.

"But you aren't?" Miss Chloe asked, brushing the debris off the table and into the garbage with her hand and then trying to dust the remaining glitter off her hand. Good luck!

"Afraid? No." I kept stacking. "I miss it." It wasn't really the forest I was talking about anymore.

"Do you?" She rubbed her glittery hands on her pants. Which naturally made her hands and her pants sparkly. "If you miss it, maybe you should go back. Unless your father or someone has directly forbidden it?"

"No, it's just the feeling I have." I shoved the stack of chairs against the wall and grabbed a broom to finish cleaning up.

"Well, Isobel, you're done with school. You're not a child. I would think you could decide for yourself what's best for you. Think about what you've actually been told and what you're assuming from the feelings you're getting."

I paused in my sweeping. Had I just assumed I couldn't return to Kilinaire? Had Leith forbidden me to return, or was it just a feeling? I'd sensed a finality to leaving, but maybe he had assumed after telling me the truth of what had happened to his sister, I wouldn't want to see him again. After all, he viewed the castle as a cursed prison, not a place someone would want to visit.

That was a lot of assuming on both sides.

"Are you all right, Isobel? Do you need me to finish up?"

"No." I started sweeping again. "Sorry, I was thinking about something."

"I'll leave you to it then." Miss Chloe patted my shoulder, and she must have left, but I didn't even register her going as I continued to mull it over. Tait and Leith had both told me the Rose Gate would only let people through with the permission of the prince. If the bear didn't want me to return, the Rose Gate would be closed.

I didn't want to come across as, well, needy. But there had been something about his expression when I left. Anyway, we were friends, right? Surely a little visit wouldn't be too much trouble? There was only one way to find out. But I had something to do first.

CHAPTER 20

I LEANED AGAINST AN ASPEN TREE AND stared at the arch of tangled roses, Lily's backpack heavy on my shoulder. It had all seemed very straightforward yesterday. Check the Rose Gate. See if I was allowed back in. But now, standing here, it didn't seem nearly so simple. What if it were open, but only because he'd forgotten to close it against me, assuming I would never come back? What if you couldn't reverse giving permission to enter, even if you wanted to?

What if he didn't want to see me again?

I don't know how long I stood there before I reached out my hand under the arch of red roses. I didn't feel anything. Was I meant to feel something? All right, this was ridiculous. I stepped forward, still half-expecting to just walk into the clearing.

What I wasn't expecting was to be hit with a blast of icy air. I gasped as snow swirled around me, whipping my hair around my face so I couldn't even see. The cold bit into my bare arms and legs as the orange-striped sundress that was perfectly comfortable in my forest proved to be utterly impractical here.

So. Cold.

Suddenly, I was enveloped in warmth as a fur-lined cloak was settled over my shoulders.

"Isobel," he said in wonder as he pulled the hood up over my hair, "you came back."

His hands fumbled the cloak's metal clasp, and I closed it myself, brushing against his scarred fingers with my own. I looked up to find him watching me.

"We should go inside," I said breathlessly. "The fish are going to freeze."

Ena started fussing as soon as I was in the castle. She lit a fire in the parlor's fireplace and bustled off to fetch hot tea. And if you've never seen a raccoon bustle, it's a bit of a sight. Leith settled me on a high-backed velvet chair with a blanket for my bare legs before sitting down on a matching settee across from me.

"You must have seen me coming in the mirror?"

Leith nodded. Oh no, he had probably watched while I stood in front of the Rose Gate for a full faerie day. How long had he been waiting there with a cloak for me?

"You said something about fish?" He sounded puzzled.

I sat up straighter and reached quickly for the bag.

"Um, yes." I felt a bit silly. "I...brought presents. To thank everyone for putting up with me while I was here."

"You brought fish?"

"For Geanan. And for Tait, I suppose." I laughed nervously. I pulled out a plastic bag with three small koi fish sloshing around in it. "I'm not sure where to put them now, though." I eyed the poor little fish dubiously. "I didn't know it would be winter already. Clearly." I wiggled my bare toes under the blanket.

"Clearly." Leith gave that half smile of his and took the bag from me. "I'm sure Ena can find a bucket of water to keep them safely in until spring."

"Ena can what?" The racoon returned with Deirdre and the tea. They set the little table with a steaming pot of tea and a basket of little cakes. "Are those fish?"

I explained the fish to her and then reached back in my bag for more gifts. A gold child's necklace for Deidre that fit perfectly around the little fox's neck and a little cardboard box for Ena.

"I didn't see any tea plants around here," I said as she opened the box of Twinings and sniffed the paper bags suspiciously. "And I didn't want my stay to have used up too much of your stores. So, I brought you some tea!"

"Did you now?" Ena lifted out a bag dubiously and watched it spin on its string. She put the bag back in the box and tucked it into the basket, then, after checking that I was warm enough, she and Deidre left the room.

I snuggled into the blanket. "I never really spent much time in here last time I was here. I guess I was outside most of the day." The snow blew against the diamond-paned glass of the windows, but the parlor was cozy. "How long have I been gone?"

"It's been three months," Leith said. "We celebrated Solstice last week."

I noticed the greenery and candles on the mantle.

"Oh, well, I guess it's good that I brought presents then. Like for Christmas! Or is it not like Christmas? Do you have Christmas?" Please, let the floor swallow me up now, if only to stop me from babbling. No one else caused me to ramble on like the fae prince did. I'm not sure anyone else in my life was quiet enough to let me try.

"It's not quite the same thing, no." He gave a half smile.

"I have something for you too. Well, it's not really a gift, but sort of…" I busied myself with digging around in my backpack to cover my treacherous blushing as I tried to stop babbling. I pulled out the worn paperback copy of *The Fellowship of the Ring* and passed it over to him.

"It's not really a gift because it's from the library, so I have to return it. But it's one of my favorite novels, and I thought that you might like to read it?"

He turned the book over in his scarred hands, and I was struck with the ridiculousness of bringing a fae prince a fantasy novel from the library. It had seemed perfect in the safety of the human world, but now I was feeling pretty silly about the idea.

"So." Leith opened the book and examined the map in the front. "This book belongs in someone's library?"

I nodded, feeling even more ridiculous.

"I suppose…" And then he looked up at me with the first full smile I had ever seen on him. It took my breath away. "I suppose that means you'll have to come back again soon to collect it."

After I finished my tea, I wrapped myself up in the fur-lined cloak, and Leith walked me back to the Rose Gate. The rest of the garden was covered in a blanket of snow, but the roses arching over the gate remained blissfully unaware of the cold. Their deep red seemed even darker against the white of the winter grounds.

"I suppose I should give this back." I reluctantly reached for the clasp on my cloak, not terribly excited to freeze again, even if it was only for a second.

"Don't be silly, *Àlainn*, there's no need to freeze you. I'll collect it on the other side." And with that he pulled my hand down from the clasp and held it firmly as he stepped through the gate, towing me behind. I barely had time to register its warmth before we were through the gate and my hand was resting on the furry shoulder of a one-eyed grizzly bear.

I had gotten so used to Leith in his fae form that I'd nearly forgotten about the bear.

"Hello, Bear," I said nervously.

The bear snuffed at me in reply.

"Oh right, here you go." I slipped out of the cloak that was definitely overkill in the July heat and handed it to the bear who gently took it in his teeth. He nodded his giant head and returned to the winter of Kilinaire.

"See you soon," I whispered to the empty air he left behind and headed back home again.

CHAPTER 21

SO, YOU DO THIS EVERY DAY, THEN? Even in the winter?"

I sat out in the courtyard where Leith was practicing sword stuff while I pretended to read. Deirdre had found me a cushion and a giant fur-lined blanket, and Rani snuggled on my lap under the blanket like a purring hot water bottle. The courtyard seemed to be spelled to keep the snow out, but I could still see my breath in the chilly afternoon air.

"It's always important to be prepared…" began Leith.

I rolled my eyes.

"A lot of dangerous beasts at Kilinaire these days?" I teased him.

"And to stay in shape."

I certainly appreciated that, even if it was sadly too cold for shirtless exercise today.

"Hmmm." I turned back to my book.

"I could teach you." Leith paused and looked my way.

"Teach me what?" I flipped a page.

"To use a sword." He sized me up critically. "Or maybe a dagger would be better."

"Is that a short joke?" I pretended to continue to read and ignore him.

"It's not a joke. You really are too short for the swords."

I shot him a look, and he laughed. The bear laughing was an unusual enough sound to capture my full attention.

"What on earth would I need to use a dagger for?" I dropped my book onto my lap, causing my lap warmer to complain under the blanket. "Not a lot of battles in Pilot Bay these days, Bear."

"And you've never been threatened by, say, vicious enchanted wolves."

"Touché. But I'm not about to start carrying weapons in my purse. It's frowned upon in Canada. You will have noticed that I'm now very careful to stay out of the woods at night. The wolves have never been seen in the daytime. No wolves, no need for daggers." I picked up my book again.

"Àlainn." Leith stalked over and plucked the book out of my cold fingers. "Humor me."

"Fine, fine," I grumbled, climbing out of my cozy blanket nest. "Sorry, Rani." The striped cat gave me a baleful glare and then stretched out with a yawn as if it had been her own idea to get up in the first place before stalking off to find a more peaceful napping location.

"It's cold, you know," I informed Leith as he pulled me by the arm over to the wall of weapons.

"Yes, Isobel, I believe it's called winter." He waved at the line of daggers. "Pick one."

I sighed and turned my attention to the weapons. Honestly, it seemed a bit reckless to just hand pointy objects to people like this, but he was obviously not going to be argued with at this point. The daggers ranged in size, and the handles were made with a variety of woods and metals. A silver blade with gold tracing the knotted designs on the handle caught my eye. It hummed at me as I picked it up.

"You're sure you want that one?"

"Why not? Is something wrong with it? Dagger choosing is not something I have a lot of experience in." I hefted it experimentally. The balance felt...like a dagger? I had no idea what it was supposed to feel like.

Leith simply held up his sword in reply. It was also silver, a larger version of the blade in my hand. They must be a set.

"Is it yours? Should I pick another one?" I offered it to him, but Leith reached out and closed my fingers around the hilt with a scarred hand.

"All the weapons are mine, Isobel," he reminded me. "This one is fine. It's a good blade. However, it's the only magical dagger on the rack. I was surprised you chose it."

"It hummed at me." I examined the dagger with greater interest. "Did the faerie who made the mirror make this as well?"

"Clíodhna?" Leith gave a bark of laughter. "Never. She doesn't believe in violence. My sword and that dagger are dwarven made. Prince Tiernan gave them to me when I joined his fianna."

"What kind of magic are they? Will this make me an expert warrior?" I brandished the dagger in the air.

"It won't. You need training for that. Please stop waving it around." Leith winced. "They're fae killers. They can break through a protective shield or pierce magically strengthened skin and put an unnatural amount of force behind the weapon. Also, most fae are sensitive to silver, so the blade itself is deadly."

"Too bad you didn't have them handy when the Unseelie Queen came to visit then."

Leith's one gray eye turned flinty. "A mistake I won't make again when I see her next."

"Are you planning to run into her?" I was trying for lightness, but something about the look on his face turned my stomach to ice. "You are planning to run into her. That's why you train every day. What are you plotting? You told me there was nothing that could be done about the curse."

"There is nothing that you can do about the curse," Leith countered. "I didn't want to burden you with my fate, not when I didn't think I'd ever see you again." He fell silent, obviously debating if he should tell me. It was exasperating.

"Before the counter-curse fails, in another few months, I'll send word to Moriath and tell her I've agreed to join her. Then when she comes, I'll take her by surprise. There are two ways to break my curse, Isobel. Either I die, or she does." He shifted his grip on the sword, eyeing the light on the blade. "And either option is fine with me."

"What?!" I squeaked. "One of those options is most definitely not fine. That's a terrible plan. You need a better plan."

"There is no better plan. Either I risk ambushing the queen, or I give in and spend the rest of my life at her side." His expression was bleak when he met my eyes at last. "Death is preferable."

"Geez, you might think so, but some of us would miss you." I knew time was running out in Kilinaire, but it hit me again, the urgency to help them. "There must be a better way. Have you actually read all those fancy books in your library? Surely one of them must have an idea on how to break a curse like this!"

"I have read them all, yes. This is the only way. Don't look so distraught, Àlainn, I'm actually pretty good with a sword." His attention turned back to my dagger. "Unlike you. You don't hold it like a bread knife, you know."

"I don't know, actually." I allowed him to change the subject. For now. But I wasn't giving up on the idea that there must be another way. "How am I supposed to hold it, then? And is it magic on its own, or does it need someone who can make it work?"

Leith set his sword down on a rack next to the daggers and came over to help me. "You hold it like this."

He adjusted my grip on the dagger. I briefly considered pretending to be clumsy to prolong the feeling of his hands on mine—it wouldn't have been much of a stretch as the grip felt unnatural—but his long fingers stilled as though I'd willed it into happening. I glanced up, surprised. We were standing so very close. His hand ran lightly over mine as his gaze held me captive. When his attention dropped to my lips, I might have swayed toward him without rational thought, but then he dropped my hand abruptly and took a step back, leaving me feeling a little lost.

What had we been talking about? I looked down at my hand. Oh, right. Daggers.

"That's better," the prince said lightly, as if nothing had happened, and I supposed nothing had. He plucked a second dagger from the rack. "Now, about the magic, it's part of the blade, but I don't know if a human could use it or not. Do you want to try?"

"Um, sure. I mean, yes. What should I do?" I gave my head a shake. Focus, Isobel.

"I'll set up a shield around the dummy." Leith stalked over to a wooden post in the center of the courtyard with a tightly stuffed bag for a head. It had clearly been the victim of many previous attacks from the nicks and gouges that covered it. "If you can get through the shield and stab the dummy, then we'll keep working with the silver dagger. If you can't, you might as well switch to an ordinary one."

I walked over and Leith demonstrated a thrust for me. Then he muttered something over the dummy and stepped back. I couldn't see anything, but I could feel that faint hum of magic coming from it.

"Okay, so I just try to stab it?" I pointed the dagger at the dummy.

"You need to do it with intent. Imagine it slicing through the shield. It can help if you picture your enemy in your mind and will the weapon to pierce the shield to hit them." He gave the dummy a pat and stepped back. "It's okay if you can't do it. We're just testing a theory."

"Right. Okay." I stepped up to the dummy and tried to imitate the stance Leith showed me. I closed my eyes and thought of my enemy. I wasn't the violent sort, but a silent rage filled me as I thought of the Unseelie Queen and all the pain she had caused the prince and the other inhabitants of Kilinaire. I focused on that thought and wielded the dagger with an enthusiasm that surprised me as I smoothly sliced through the enchanted shield and hit the dummy with enough magical force that the imaginary queen's head exploded into a rain of straw and sawdust.

I stumbled back, and Leith and I both stared open-mouthed at the dagger stuck halfway through the post.

"Well." I wiped my clammy hands on my pants. "I think I'll stick with the magic dagger."

CHAPTER 22

THERE MIGHT BE NOTHING IN Leith's library that would help break the curse, but I couldn't believe books would let us down completely. After exhausting Pilot Bay's meager offerings on the subject, I took my search online. I didn't have the cash for books, but luckily the library was in a network with other libraries across British Columbia, giving me access to a couple of million books.

Obviously, most of these were useless, but I ordered in a handful that looked promising. I didn't mention it to Leith. I knew it was a long shot that any human books would contain the secrets of fae magic, but our worlds were linked through the gates, so anything was possible.

It took a few days for them to start arriving, but one afternoon when I was busy organizing the kids' books from that day's reading club, Miss Chloe set a stack of books down on the counter beside me.

"*Modern Witchcraft and Curses*," she read, picking up the first book. She glanced at the titles underneath. "*Hexes For Any Occasion? He's Just Not That Into You, So Turn Him Into a Frog?*" She squinted at the last one before looking up at me. "Isobel? Your recent book choices are a bit unusual. What would Pastor Brian say?"

I scrambled for a reasonable explanation. School paper? No wait, I wasn't in school anymore. Could I say I was writing a novel? I could be writing a novel. "I...um..." I hazarded a glance at Miss Chloe. The head librarian was trying hard to look concerned, but there was a mischievous twinkle in her eye she was failing to control. Something clicked in my brain.

"You!" I dropped the picture book I'd been scanning in. "You know something!"

"About *Transformation and Shrinkification?* I should hope not." Miss Chloe cracked the book open and flipped to the table of contents. "Why would anyone want to turn themselves into a newt?" She tapped her chin thoughtfully. "Actually, now that I come to think of it..."

"It was you who told me to go to the miner's cabin. You don't even hike!"

"These old knees, you know." She continued to read the book, clearly trying not to make eye contact with me.

"How old are your old knees exactly?" I narrowed my eyes at her.

"Really, Isobel, what a shocking question. And so loud too," she murmured.

"You're one of them, aren't you?" I hissed more quietly.

"One of whom? Librarians? Senior citizens? Fans of the Marvel Extended Universe?"

"Fae." The word dropped between us into the silent library.

Miss Chloe snapped the book on hexes shut and set it on top of the pile. "I'm sure I can't have this conversation without a hot cup of tea. Time for some Pie in the Sky, I think." And with that she pulled her purse off the hook by the office door. "Shall we?" And off she went through the big glass library doors, leaving me staring after her with the book scanner still in my upraised hand. She popped her head back into the library. "Don't forget your spell books!"

A half hour later I was no closer to any sort of answers, but I did have a chai latte and a slice of apple pie was on its way, so it wasn't a total loss. Miss Chloe sipped her tea cheerfully as the server came with our pastries.

"Thank you, Neve," said Miss Chloe warmly to the girl, as if they were old friends. Then again, the librarian seemed to know everyone. The server was plump and pretty with pale skin and her black hair tied up in a red scarf and colorful tattoos up one arm. Her style reminded me of a vintage pin-up girl.

"Weren't you in my biology class?" I asked her.

"I think so." Neve set the slices of pie down on the pretty shabby chic café table. "I was in grade eleven last year, but I took some senior classes to try and graduate early. Small town, right? You start to know everyone."

"Or at least you think you do." I turned back to Miss Chloe as the girl went to check on another table. "What do you have to say for yourself?"

"So many, many things." Miss Chloe peacefully took another sip of tea. "I just love a table by the window. Don't you? So many interesting people in this town."

"Are you fae?" I chose to ignore her ridiculous small talk.

"I am, yes."

Even though I knew it already, I felt a shiver go down my spine at her words.

"Why do you look like a human? Why are you living in Pilot Bay? What do you know about Leith and the Rose Gate?"

"Glamour in the glasses." Miss Chloe tapped her gold frames. "Pretty good, right? I'm not actually nearsighted. My true form would draw a bit too much unwanted attention." She reached for her fork, but I pulled the pie away from her.

"You said we would talk. Talk first, then pie."

"You human children, always in such a hurry." She sighed. "All right, all right, where to start...?"

"Leith," I suggested. She cocked an eyebrow at me.

"Leith, then. You asked me earlier, very impertinently, I might add, how old I was. I've known the family at Kilinaire since Leith's grandfather was a baby, and that's as much as I'll admit to. I've been something of a faerie godmother to the young Rose Court heirs for generations. My home is in the woods a few leagues to the south of theirs. I watch over many young people of influence in Tír na nÓg, but Kilinaire has always taken much of my attention. It's so close to the Unseelie court that it's hard for Moriath to keep her claws away from it.

"Back in Leith's grandfather's day, the fae tended to visit other parts of the human world. Places with traditions of music and art drew them. They would go among the humans to hear their stories and songs and sometimes steal the most talented away to amuse the *Tuatha Dé Danann* in the courts. The oldest faerie gates are in places far from your young mountains here."

"Like Ireland." I remembered what Leith had told me.

"Amongst others, yes. The Rose Gate in particular was often connected to that part of the world. But then, as time sped along in your world, precious metals were discovered in North America. The fae are always hungry for gold and silver. Gold to make the most potent magical objects and silver to craft the deadliest weapons. They built gates here, in British Columbia, during the gold rush to get as much as possible."

"There's more than one gate near here?" I asked, surprised. One local portal to a faerie realm seemed like plenty.

"There are three within walking distance of town," she confirmed. "And more throughout the region. The gates are the only way of traveling between our worlds, so when gold was discovered here, both of the courts sent craftsmen through the closest gates, and they traveled across your world to set up gates. It was quite a race, actually, not unlike the human gold rush. The dwarves got here first, naturally."

"Naturally," I agreed, as if I knew all about the ways of dwarves.

"And so, for a time there was quite a bit of traffic between the realms, but of course the mines were eventually exhausted. The fae lost interest, and indeed, most of the humans left the area, too. Now all that's left in the region are a few small towns, a handful of ghost towns, and a smattering of faerie gates."

"They just left the gates? That seems…"

"Untidy?" suggested Miss Chloe over a sip of tea.

"I was going to say dangerous." I ate another bite of the excellent apple pie. "Aren't they afraid people will wander through?"

"The gates can't be destroyed easily, but they were sealed. And even minor gates can't be opened without more skill and intention than a wandering human would possess."

"Okay, so that explains the gates, but what does that have to do with Leith and the curse at Kilinaire?"

"As I mentioned, Moriath has been a problem for some time. There are things that need to be dealt with in the Unseelie Court."

"It sounds as though the Seelie Court has some issues too." Leith, at least, was awfully suspicious of King Fiachra.

"True enough." Miss Chloe eyed me with interest. "The time has come for things to start shifting. The mess with Leith and Neala taught me that, while I have the advantage of experience, Moriath has the advantage of power. There is only so much that can be done if you're not willing to fuel your magic at the expense of others."

"You were the Elder Fae who helped Neala free Leith from Moriath's influence?"

"For what good it did, yes. But then Moriath used his broken vow and that poor girl's blood to cast an even stronger curse."

"But you cast the counter-curse to protect Leith and the others at Kilinaire."

"Which has nearly run out, as you've seen."

"What can be done then?" My fork fell to the plate with a clatter. "If you don't have enough power, and no one else will help, what hope is there?"

"Oh, there is always hope. What do you think I'm here for?" asked Miss Chloe, cheerfully. "Other than the cafés, of course." She took a bite of pie. "Those who want to control others always think power is all that's needed. And it works for a while. But they underestimate what can be done by people who truly care for each other."

"So, what are you trying to say?"

"These things have a way of working themselves out."

"That's your plan?" I was getting too annoyed to even enjoy my pie. "That things will work themselves out?"

"And it's going brilliantly so far. Don't you worry." Miss Chloe smiled as she poured another cup of tea.

"But she's still an evil queen! Leith is still cursed! We don't have a way to stop her."

"Not all of those problems are yours to worry about."

I glared at the head librarian wordlessly.

"Oh, don't be so grumpy." She laughed. "Here, have some more pie."

CHAPTER 23

T HE NEXT TIME I ARRIVED AT KILINAIRE I had
questions, sage, and scissors. When I stepped
through the Rose Gate, Leith raised an eyebrow at
the look of determination on my face.

"Turn around three times and spit," I demanded by
way of greeting.

"What?"

I just made a twirling motion with my hand, so he
shrugged and turned around three times on the stone
path before spitting into the snow-dusted hedge. I held
my breath. Nope, nothing.

"Well, that's not it." I hefted my bag onto my shoulders. "I was thinking," I said, picking my way through the
slushy path toward the castle steps, "that you might like a
haircut."

"I would like a haircut, yes." Leith jogged a step to catch up to me before falling in beside my determined stride. "Are you planning on telling me what the spitting was about?"

"It's a way to break curses. Apparently not all of them though. I've been doing some research." I stopped on the steps and looked back at the dormant rose garden. "I know it's a long shot I'll find anything, but it can't hurt, right?"

"Isobel." He brushed his dark, ragged bangs back. "Just don't get your hopes up." He sighed and looked at me for a long moment. He opened his mouth and then paused.

"Yes?" Hopefully my reply wasn't too breathless.

"Do you even know how to cut hair?"

The concern in his gray eye was real.

I patted his arm. "Let's find out together, shall we?"

"Now." I eyed my new scissors speculatively. "I haven't actually cut anyone's hair before, no."

Leith turned to give me a look from the short kitchen stool where he sat in front of me, wrapped in a sheet to protect his clothes.

"However," I continued hastily, "I have watched five different YouTube videos on it."

"I have no idea what that is." Leith did not sound reassured.

"And Lily has been cutting Dad's hair since we left Vancouver, so it can't be that hard, right?" It would have been easier if I could have asked Lily how to do it, but that would have raised more questions than I was willing to answer right now. "Turn your head back around, and I'll get started."

Leith just looked at me.

"Oh, come on, Bear, it'll grow back. And I can't possibly do a worse job than this hacking at it with a knife business you've been doing." I put my hand on top of his head and turned it back to face the kitchen. The ever-present beavers had fled at the rare sight of their master in their domain, but Ena was bustling about, and Tait was observing the proceedings with great interest. I untied the leather strap that held Leith's hair back and pulled at the cord that held his patch on. His hand darted up and caught mine.

"It's okay. I can't cut hair around it. And anyway, I've seen you without the patch before."

"And you ran away screaming," he reminded me evenly.

I winced. I had done that. "I won't scream today. I'm not afraid of the scary bear anymore." I gave his rough hand a squeeze and pulled my fingers away to finish removing the patch. After setting it on the table beside me, I gathered his hair in my hand and cut the ponytail off in one snip. Tait gasped loudly from across the table. Hmm, these scissors were pretty sharp.

"Just watch the ears, please," Leith begged with a wince.

"Oh, don't worry, no fae-to-human plastic surgery today." I started cutting the back like the videos had shown, trimming the hair a finger's width from the back of his head. I cut in silence. I hadn't thought through how very close and…touchy hair cutting would be. The memory of our almost-kiss burned in my mind, although neither of us mentioned it.

"So, you used to have short hair?" Good, not at all awkward. Right. "I always pictured fae men with long, flowing, elfy hair. Not that I sat around picturing fae men…" Better and better, Isobel.

"I found it easier under a helmet." Leith relaxed slightly. Hopefully he was trusting that I really wouldn't chop his ear tips off with the scissors. "Most courtiers prefer long hair, but even when I left the Fianna, I could never get used to it long. It gets in the way."

"Hmm, I've never had mine short, but I guess I can see what you mean." I snipped his dark hair to make an even line above his pale neck. Okay, it was nearly even. He wouldn't be able to see the back of his neck anyway. "I'm surprised you didn't learn to cut it yourself."

"I didn't know how to cut my hair when I had two good eyes. Wielding scissors with only one seemed like a bad idea. It took me over a year to pour my own tea without missing the cup. That didn't bode well for something involving scissors."

I'd never considered what it must have been like for Leith to adjust to losing his eye. "Was it hard to get used to only seeing out of one side?"

"It's not only about how much I can see, although that was affected. With only one eye it can be hard to judge distances. Things are never quite where you think they are."

Leith's daily sword training took on a new light. That must make it difficult to hit a target.

Ena set a steaming cup on the long table beside us.

"I made the…tea…you brought today," said Ena with a doubtful sniff. "If you can call it that."

"It smells like rotting snakes," added Tait helpfully.

"Hush, phouka." I gave my friend a look. "Or I'll make you drink it too. Besides, I'm sure it won't be too bad with a bit of honey."

Ena herded a reluctant Tait out of the kitchen, leaving Leith to my mercy. I sniffed the tea and made a face. Tait might have a point.

"For you." I pushed the teacup down the table toward the prince.

"Why?" he asked, sniffing the tea. "What have I ever done to you to deserve this?"

"It's white sage, comfrey, hyssop, hemlock, and nettle. Sadly, the Pilot Bay Health Food Store didn't have any feverfew." I gave another snip. "Also, some sea salt."

Leith took a sip and spat most of it out on the floor. "Just set the wolves on me again if you're trying to kill me!"

I continued to cut. The back of his hair was quite short now, but the rest was still long and uneven. Like a really ugly reverse mullet. Oh, for a camera.

"They're all herbs that are supposed to break curses," I said with a sigh. "I know, it's silly, but…I wanted to try. It kills me to not try. But I don't know if there's anything written in my world that would even help. Can magic even exist there? All the books seem to talk about being cursed with bad luck or things like that, but I've never really believed in that sort of thing. And the more earnest the books seemed, the creepier they got. I ended up returning them all."

I trimmed carefully around his left ear. Jokes aside, I really didn't want to snip the point off. Imagine the blood. No, don't imagine the blood.

"As far as I know, magic doesn't exist naturally in your world." Leith eyed his teacup suspiciously as he spoke. "Objects of power can be brought into your world, and the magic stored in them would still be present, but they can't be created there."

"So how do the gates work in my world, then?" I finished up one side with no ear damage and got to work on the other.

"Exactly how the gates work is beyond my understanding of magic. But I do know that when they create the gates, they have to bring gold ingots infused with the spell to your world and bury them under the gate. That powers the gate on your end."

"Huh. Like a magical battery." I started to cut on top, leaving the hair a bit longer than the sides.

"I suppose?" He was silent while I steadily snipped the hair on top of his head, brushing the loose strands to the floor periodically. "If you didn't believe in curses and magic, what did you believe in?"

"Not faeries, either." I gave a half laugh. "God, prayer. Angels and demons. I thought the rest were all only stories."

"And have you prayed for me?" Leith asked cautiously. "Or are you just subjecting me to terrible tea?"

I finished up the back of his head in silence, then I moved around to finish the front of his hair. I was surprised to see how vulnerable he looked as he waited for my answer.

"I've been praying for you since I met you," I said finally. I trimmed his hair and brushed it across his forehead to see how it lay. This part was trickier than I'd expected. I narrowed my eyes and took a bit off one side.

"And yet, here I still am, curse and all." Leith looked down at his hands. "I don't think your prayers will have any more effect than the spitting did."

"Because you don't believe God exists?" I studied my work. It wasn't perfect, but it was pretty good. And Leith looked more than pretty good with his hair short. I felt a tightness in my chest as I took in how it sharpened his strong features and the line of his cheekbones.

"Because he knows I've received only what I deserve." Leith brought his gaze up to mine, half his face the ruin he believed himself to be. But I could see so much more than that.

All my words caught in my throat until he reached for the teacup again, and the moment passed. He took another sip and grimaced. "So, *Àlainn.*"

"Hmm?" I brushed the hair off his shoulders, pretending it wasn't an excuse to touch him. There was enough hair on the ground to create a friend for Rani.

"Do you have any other curse-breaking plans for me today? Should I brace myself? Run, perhaps?"

"I do have one more thing, actually." I dug through my backpack on the table before producing a ziplock full of salt and other things. I plunked it down beside the teacup. "Take a bath with this in it during the next full moon. It, um, might sting a little."

"Sounds perfect to me."

While I was sweeping up the hair, Deirdre and Tait appeared with a hand mirror in a basket. Leith put his patch back in place. Happily, he couldn't see the back of his head in the mirror as he pronounced his haircut to be perfect. I shouldered my pack, and Leith rose to walk me out while the otter and fox cleared up the remains of the useless tea. I heard a loud crash and a yelp behind us, and

I turned back to see Tait howling, surrounded by broken porcelain and shards of mirrored glass.

I ran back, picking my way through the dainty shrapnel. Tait was bleeding from a nasty slice on his front leg.

"Honestly, Tait," scolded Deirdre, "if I had a copper for every time you've broken a dish while helping..."

I gently lifted Tait out of the mess and set him on the table. His howls quieted to sniffles as I examined the injury. Ooh. That looked like it would need stitches.

Leith bent down beside me and hovered his hand above the cut leg. The hairs on the back of my arms stood up as the humming sensation I had come to identify as magic at work built in the air.

"Wait!" I grabbed Leith's wrist. Both the prince and the otter stared at me in surprise. "Can I try?"

"What?" squeaked Tait.

"If I could make the magic in the dagger work, does that mean I could do small magic, like you all can? I mean, it's worth a shot, right?"

"I'm not sure I feel comfortable with this." The little otter sounded surprisingly strong all of a sudden.

Leith stared at my hand on his wrist, and I quickly let go. "It's not quite the same thing," he mused. "The dagger had the magic in it. To heal, you need to pull the magic of Faerie to yourself and channel it. I'm not sure if it will work, but you may try if you'd like."

"But I'm injured," protested Tait. "It could be tricky. Shouldn't she start with something easier? Like a nice levitation spell?"

"We can try that after." I patted his head.

"I didn't mean on me!"

"Hold your hand here." Leith moved my hand gently, positioning it above the injury. "Small magic, remember, is mostly a matter of intention. Think of what you want to accomplish and feel what magic you have in the surrounding area."

I closed my eyes. The weight of Leith's hand over mine was distracting, but I focused on my desire to heal my friend. I could feel the buzzing in the air around me, but faintly. It didn't feel focused. "Now what?"

"Now you put your intention into words. We always use *Gaeilge Arsa*, the language you said sounds like Irish. But I don't know if that's because the language itself is important, or if saying the words in your birth language holds more weight."

"Okay, what would I say in Galgi whatsit?"

"So not reassuring," whimpered Tait.

Leith spoke slowly in lilting syllables, and I repeated his inflection as best I could, but nothing happened.

"Good try, Isobel." Tait started to get up. "You probably just need to practice for a bit first. With something less...sentient."

"No, wait. Let me try one more time."

Tait sighed and laid back down.

I closed my eyes and felt the magic around me in the air again. "Be healed." I put as much belief and intention into the words as I could. The humming intensified until I felt like my bones must be vibrating. Then it resolved with a popping feeling. I opened one eye to see Leith's hand still over mine. I pulled my hand away and peeked at Tait's leg. It was fully healed.

"I did it!" I scooped Tait up and gave him a tight squeeze. "I healed you!"

"And you'll have to heal me again if you don't loosen your arms a bit!" gasped the little otter.

"I did it." I beamed at Leith.

"You did," he agreed.

"I was so sure it wouldn't work for me because I'm not fae." I set the squirming otter a clean patch of floor.

"Honestly, I didn't think you'd be able to do it either." Leith pretended to ignore me as I smacked his arm.

"What?!" squeaked Tait.

"Shhhh." I patted him on the head. "All's well that ends well. I'm sure what you're trying to say is 'Thank you, Isobel.'"

Tait kept shooting me murderous looks as Leith walked me out of the room again.

"What else can you teach me to do?" I was practically bouncing beside Leith as we reached the Rose Gate again.

"I'm really not sure I'm the best person to be teaching you magic," admitted Leith. "Most of my expertise is only useful in battle. If you want more weapons practice, I'm happy to help."

"What? You don't want to teach me the magic trick with the hair ribbon?" I teased.

"Not really my best talent, no." Leith gave a laugh at my obvious excitement. "I wish I could ask Clíodhna for help, but cut off as we are from the rest of Faerie…"

"Wait." I stopped and grabbed his arm. "I forgot to tell you."

"Tell me what?"

"Miss Chloe is the Elder Fae!" I waited for his shocked and amazed outburst. It didn't come.

"Who?" He stared at me.

"Miss Chloe. The head librarian!"

"Your head librarian is an Elder Fae?" He put a hand to my forehead which I swatted away.

"Yes, yes! I'm not delirious, she's Clíodhna. She's been in my world since the curse started. I think she's trying to work undercover from there, although, to be honest, she's not been terribly helpful. She might just be staying for the Avengers movies."

Leith had obviously tuned out my babbling. "Clíodhna in the human world, all this time," he muttered to himself. "I have much to think about, Isobel." He patted my shoulder absentmindedly, then turned and headed back down the path, lost in thought.

Not the reaction I'd been expecting, but that was okay. I was still buzzing with the happiness of healing my friend. With magic! What else could I do?

CHAPTER 24

BLUEBERRIES OR CHOCOLATE CHIP?" Lily greeted me as I came down the stairs for breakfast.

"Is that a real question? Of course, chocolate. Always chocolate." I yawned, hefting the kettle from the stove experimentally. It was still full enough from Lily's coffee, so I turned the stove element on and blearily rummaged through boxes of tea for something with caffeine.

"But when I make chocolate chip pancakes the chocolate melts and burns in the pan." Lily eyed her mixing bowl with a frown. "I should probably make blueberry."

"Then why are you even asking me?" I found a bag of Earl Grey and left it in my favorite blue mug while I waited for the water to boil. "Where's Dad and Amber?"

"Dad's at work already—yes, on a Saturday—and Amber is sleeping, I assume."

Dad took as many shifts as he could. I was never sure if it was because we needed the money, or if he was actually avoiding us. It certainly wasn't for the love of pumping gas.

The phone rang, and Lily waved at it with her wooden spoon. "Can you grab that?"

I dutifully picked up the receiver. "Hello?"

"Hello, little girl." The voice was male, and yes, super creepy. It was too early for creepy. "Please let me speak with your father."

"He's not available right now." Something about that voice made me unwilling to admit my dad wasn't home. Not that he offered much protection. "Can I take a message?"

"Please remind him that all debts must be accounted for. I'll talk to him soon."

The line went dead, and I gave the phone a confused look before hanging up and going back into the kitchen. My water was boiling, so I poured it into my mug. "Lily?"

"Hmm?" She pulled her favorite cast iron pan out and moved her bowl over to the stove.

"When Dad declared bankruptcy, they wiped out all his debts, right?" I dunked my tea bag up and down, watching the dark stain spread through the water.

"Basically, yeah, why?" She held her hand over the pan to test the heat.

"Some weird guy just called and said something about Dad's debts. But he shouldn't have any debts." I squished the last inky drops out of the bag, burning my fingers in the process before squeezing in some honey from the nearly empty plastic bear.

"I answered a call like that last week." She looked up at me with a worried expression. "I told Dad, but he brushed it off. I don't know what's up."

"You don't think he did anything illegal, do you?"

"Like what?" Lily watched a pat of butter melt in the pan, giving it a swirl.

"Gambling? Or the mob? Does Vancouver have a mob?"

Amber slumped onto the bar stool next to me and pillowed her head on her arms, apparently too tired to make eye contact. "Is there coffee?" she moaned. "Are those chocolate chip pancakes?" She perked up a little.

"Blueberry," Lily told her. "And there's coffee on the counter." *Later*, she mouthed at me over Amber's semi-comatose form. "So." She scooped batter into the pan with a sizzle. "Who has plans for today? I thought we might take a picnic to the beach for supper."

"Sure." I took a sip of life-giving tea. "I was going to go for a hike this morning, but I'll be home by then."

Amber pushed herself up off the counter to roll her eyes at me. "Always with the hiking! If you're trying to lose weight, you should cut carbs, like me."

"I'm not trying to lose weight. I just like hiking. It's peaceful."

"By which you mean boring. Maybe I'll come along and keep you company. You can show me that cabin thing. Do you think it would be a good place for a bush party?"

Lily put a cup of coffee in front of Amber and received no gratitude, of course.

"I have no idea. And no thanks, I want some time to myself."

"Because you're weird." Amber sipped her coffee with a contented sigh.

"Because you're annoying," I retorted.

"No pancakes for people who argue at breakfast," proclaimed Lily, setting a stack of fluffy, golden perfection in front of each of us. "Or are you not eating carbs again, Amber?"

"Pancake carbs don't count." Amber dug in happily. "And I can always hike them off later with Bel."

I glared at her, but she smiled back sweetly. I knew she was just trying to push my buttons, but I would have to be careful. The last thing I needed was Amber getting too curious and following me.

After breakfast, I grabbed the library book I had checked out for Leith and left for the forest. By which I mean that I snuck out while Amber was in the bathroom. We were into August now, and the forest was hot even in the morning. The grass was full of grasshoppers that

213

snapped and crackled as I hiked, but the treetops were growing quieter as all the birds either migrated through or settled down with their mates for the summer.

The ferns on the edge of the forest had grown waist high, and I felt like I was wading through them as they leaned into the path. When I reached the gate, I paused to pull on my cardigan. It was already early spring at Kilinaire, but it could still be cold there. Unlike the Kootenays where I was sweating. With barely a glance at the miner's cabin in the clearing, I stepped through the gate.

And was plunged into darkness.

I stood there blinking as my eyes adjusted to the starlight. While I was growing used to the fast movement of seasons in Faerie, it hadn't occurred to me to think about the time of day. It felt a bit silly to be standing there in the dark garden. Everyone must be sleeping inside. I should probably come back in an hour? Half an hour? I really wasn't sure, and time didn't flow at a predictable speed between the worlds. I'd decided to just go home when I heard the heavy wooden door to the castle open and close in the distance. I turned back to find Leith walking down the stairs, barefoot on the cold stone.

"I'm sorry!" I whispered, meeting him halfway down the path. "Did I wake you up?"

The lack of shoes and the way his dark hair stuck up endearingly in the back answered my question for me.

"It's fine." He yawned, then reached out for my hand. I stared at it for a beat, my small tanned fingers against his scarred winter-pale hand. I looked up, and he smiled, that true smile I still saw so rarely it took my breath away. "It's fine," he repeated. "Come, I want to show you something."

He led me through the castle, silent but for our soft footsteps. We went up the stairs to the library, dimly lit by candles that burst into flames a few steps ahead of us—I had to learn to do that!— and then up another flight of spiral stairs past a doorway that must lead to his living area. He paused, but instead of going in, he let me go past him through an arched doorway that led to the outside of the tower. I stepped through hesitantly, wondering how far off the ground we were now, and found more stairs. These wound around the outside of the tower, happily with a waist-high stone wall between me and the empty air. No candles lit the steps out here, but the stars gave enough light to see by.

"Only a little farther." Leith was just behind me. His hand felt hot against my back until I stepped away from him and up the steps. "I've been thinking about what you said, about Clíodhna. Would you ask her to come with you next time? I have many questions for her."

"You're not the only one." I climbed carefully, my hand trailing on the smooth top of the carved stone wall. I couldn't make out the designs on it. The swirling carved shapes kept their secrets in the shadows. "I'll talk to her at work on Monday."

The top of the stairs opened onto a wide balcony that ran around the last bit of the tower. The top of the tower was more like a gazebo with wide arched doorways on each side and a tall pointed roof above. Between the doorways, curved stone benches wrapped around the outer walls of the tower. Small trees, barely leafing out, stood in pots, and unsurprisingly, climbing roses covered half of the walls. It must be amazing up here when they bloomed.

I pulled my cardigan closer against the cool night air and walked over to the stone wall. I could see all of Kilinaire from up here, the formal patterns of the rose garden, the bare trees in the orchard, the peaks and valleys of the castle roof. Even in the night I could see the blurred horizon where the protective bubble around the castle ended. Although it was hard to see exactly where it was in the dark, it had obviously grown closer. I felt a flutter of panic, the memory of Neala's scream in the smothering darkness pressing in on me, but then Leith leaned over beside me and settled his elbows on the wall. His arm pressed lightly against mine, and the warmth brought me back to the calm of the dark night.

"Your stars are so different from ours." I took in the strange sky. "And so bright, although that could be because I live close to town. Even in a small town it's hard to see the stars." A vast display of winking lights looked down on us. "I never really thought about it before, but you can see the sky clearly from here. The barrier must be a cylinder, not a dome."

"It's true," he answered. "And I'm thankful for it. I think we'd all go mad if we couldn't see the sky. I come up here often when I can't sleep. Looking at the stars makes me remember that we are truly still in Tír na nÓg, even if it doesn't feel like it."

"Can the faeries who were transformed into birds fly out?" I wondered.

"They can, but they remain birds even beyond the edge of the curse." He turned to look at me, his hair inky dark against the stars. "No terrible concoctions for me to drink today? I hope you haven't given up on me." He said the last bit lightly, as if his time weren't quickly running out.

"Never." I leaned my arm against his. I had spent my free time reading yet another stack of unhelpful books and was about ready to give up on the library as a source of magical information, but I hadn't given up on the idea that there was something I could do to help.

After that, our talk turned to other things. I told him stories about the little kids at reading club, and he filled me in on Tait's latest attempt to impress the bunny maids— sadly unsuccessful. We talked until the sky showed hints of morning light and Leith's yawns started to make me feel guilty for keeping him up half the night.

"I'm sorry I woke you," I said one more time as Leith walked me to the Rose Gate. "How did you know I was here if you were sleeping?"

"I can tell if someone goes through the gate. It's part of the spell. It woke me up."

"Like a doorbell? Or a security system?" I stopped in front of the arching roses. They were tightly closed for the night but still heavy with flowers even when the rest of the garden still slept.

"I don't know what either of those are, but yes, probably." He reached past me and broke a rose from the vine. "While I was happy to see you tonight, it would be useful for you to be able to judge the time of day." He offered me the rose. "As you seem set on continuing to visit."

"I am." I took the rose gingerly, minding the wicked-looking thorns. His hand brushed the back of mine and then was gone.

"The roses from the gate will continue to open and close with the sunlight, even when separated from it. This should make it easier for you to judge the time of day before you come."

"Like the roses on my side of the gate?" I should have clued into that sooner. The roses must have been closed for the night when I stepped through the gate.

"Those roses have grown through the gate over the years. They seem to go where they like, even if they're still linked to Kilinaire."

"Like Rani?" Ena had mentioned the cat came and went without regard for curses or boundaries.

Leith laughed. "Exactly. The roses carry magic all their own after centuries of edging the gate. And I used a bit more of Kilinaire's magic to ensure this one won't wilt, not as long as the castle remains."

I examined the rose with interest.

"Goodnight, *Àlainn*," he added, with a yawn to emphasize his point.

"Goodnight, Bear." I took one last look at the stars twinkling above before I stepped through the gate into the blinding sunshine of my forest.

I closed my eyes briefly against the brightness, then opened them to see the rose in my hand slowly unfurling as morning broke in the castle. I had seen enchanted mirrors and talking otters, but this felt more magical than anything I had experienced. It was like watching one of those stop-motion nature documentaries, but with none of the jerky movements or changing light. It was simply magic. When the rose was fully opened, I breathed in its heady scent and stepped through the gate once more.

Leith stood there in the full sunshine of early afternoon. "Why didn't you go home?" he asked. "Is something the matter with the rose? I…"

I ran the two steps between us and caught him in a hug. He stood stiffly still for a breath and then tentatively wrapped his arms around me. He was so much taller than me, my head barely reached his chest.

"Thank you for the magic rose, Bear." I broke away and ran back to the gate, turning at the last moment to see the stunned expression on the fae prince's face before I jumped home again.

CHAPTER 25

LEITH WANTS TO TALK TO YOU," I said, plopping down into an office chair beside Miss Chloe's. It spun gently under my weight. I had a few minutes before I needed to set up for reading club, and I intended to spend them convincing my fae friend to be a bit more helpful.

"Does he now?" Miss Chloe didn't look up from her keyboard as she efficiently hunted and pecked at an email. "I've always liked Leith. Such a nice boy."

"If you say so." I tried to imagine Leith as a nice boy instead of a surly one-eyed bear man.

"But, sadly, no, I can't go talk with him." She peered over the glasses on the end of her nose and then pushed them up and tried looking through them instead.

"Why not?" I asked, exasperated. "Do you have pressing library business? How could that possibly be more important than helping your godson and the rest of the faeries trapped at Kilinaire?"

"Isobel." Miss Chloe tapped a few more lines before sending her email and turning to me. "The protection of knowledge and the education of children are always important."

I restrained the urge to roll my eyes. "But is it urgently needing your attention this afternoon?"

"It is not, but I still can't go."

"Why not?"

"I can't go back to Tír na nÓg until Moriath is defeated. She's a bit annoyed with me."

"For messing with Leith's curse?"

"Amongst other things. I'm only still alive because she hasn't thought to look for me here." Miss Chloe tapped her gold-rimmed glasses meaningfully. "Anyway, direct interference from me at this point wouldn't be helpful." She picked up an empty teacup and gave it a disappointed look before setting it back down on her desk.

"Please explain how helping would not be helpful." I sighed and stared at the ceiling, turning slowly as my chair rotated.

"I've already given you everything you need to figure this out. You don't need any further assistance."

"So, we already have what we need to break the curse?"

"Precisely."

"And where exactly are these magical curse-breaking items?" I wasn't expecting a direct answer by this point.

"In your hearts."

"Really, Miss Chloe?" I wailed. "In our hearts? What am I, some sort of magical chosen one?" I sat up in my chair and stopped spinning. "Wait, am I?"

"Hmm." Miss Chloe tapped her chin. "It rather depends on your definition. You're no more magical than any other human, I'm afraid. As for you being chosen, I'm not sure it matters. Is it more useful to be chosen and not know it, or to not be chosen but still be the one who's needed? If you break the curse, then with the perspective of the future, you are the chosen one, I suppose. But only if you succeed."

I was growing more and more convinced that she was deliberately trying to make me crazy. "So, I'm only the one who's meant to break the spell if I break the spell?"

"Would you rather have no free will?"

"How did this turn into a religious debate?"

"Excellent question. You should probably continue this discussion with your pastor." Miss Chloe turned back to her computer.

"Will everything actually turn out fine?" I asked her softly, getting up to leave.

"There is a very good possibility of that."

Not as reassuring as one might hope.

That afternoon, I timed my visit by watching my rose unfurl as I walked through the forest. Even without Miss Chloe along, I was still eager to see Leith again. I didn't know what the future held for us, but I felt like something was growing between us during my last few visits.

I stepped through the gate and found the garden empty. No fae prince waiting for me. Where was he?

Spring was making itself felt at Kilinaire, with all the roses budding and the honeybees waking and lazily buzzing about. It looked like something out of a dream, but my stomach felt like lead as I walked down the path to the castle. I must be overreacting. He was probably busy with the bees or something. I opened the castle doors to an empty room. No sign of Leith or anyone else. As I went up the steps, I nearly tripped over the sassy rabbits polishing the floor, which relieved the knot in my chest a little bit. Things must not be too much out of the ordinary. But where was Leith?

Hesitantly, I climbed the tower to the library. It was just as empty and peaceful as the rest of the castle, so I continued to the next level and was confronted with the closed wooden door to Leith's suite. I stared at it. Knock? Bad idea?

I knocked twice. The sound echoed in the silent tower.

"Leave me," came Leith's voice sharply through the door.

"Um, it's Isobel," I called back. "I have a book for you?"

"Isobel." His tone was distant. "Please go."

"But I have the next Shadowhunter book here for you!" I tried to sound casual. I didn't know if it worked. "I mean, after the cliffhanger the last book ended on, surely you…"

"You need to leave, *Àlainn*," he interrupted gruffly.

"I could get Ena to make you a cup of tea and…"

"Did you not hear me the first three times?"

His tone made the knot in my chest turn into a sharp pain.

"But…"

"Go. Away."

My eyes stung with tears, and I turned and ran down the stairs before I started crying. I didn't want to give him the satisfaction of hearing me cry.

I hardly saw the garden, the bright sunshine mocking me as I dashed back to the Rose Gate.

"Isobel! My dear girl, please wait."

I turned and rubbed my face with the back of my hand as Ena scampered down the castle steps and caught up with me.

"The prince," she began, panting a little.

"Doesn't want to see me." I willed my voice to be steady even though I knew my eyes were puffy and my face was blotchy. Some girls look beautiful when they cry, but I'm not one of them.

"No, you don't understand, he…"

"He was perfectly clear." I turned to leave again. I had obviously misjudged what was building between us. I thought we were friends, but maybe he didn't see me the same way.

"It's not about you." Ena ran around me and stood in front of me on the path. "It's Neala."

"His sister?" I asked in a watery voice.

"Yes, her." Ena wrung her paws together. "This is the anniversary of the curse. This is the day we all turned into animals, and it's the day…"

"When she died," I finished softly.

"Yes."

"Does that mean he gets to talk to me like he did?"

"Sometimes when we are hurting, we can hurt those around us without intending to," said the raccoon. "I know he values your friendship. Please don't let him drive you away. He needs you more than he would ever admit."

I held my rose tighter in my hand. "I think I understand."

Ena sighed with relief.

"But I hope he understands that he needs to apologize if he wants me to visit again."

With that, I walked around Ena and left Kilinaire behind me.

CHAPTER 26

I WAS A TOUCH OUT OF SORTS for the next few days. I wasn't a very nice sister. I wasn't a very nice daughter. I did my best to be a good teacher at library club, but I gave Miss Chloe more than her fair share of stink eyes.

I was grouchy with Leith for being a jerk, but I was equally grouchy with myself for letting it get to me so badly. I wasn't the sort of girl to get all tied in a knot about whether some boy liked her or not. Although perhaps referring to a hundreds-years-old fae prince as a boy was a bit of a stretch.

I went back and forth between anger that he had been so rude to me and worry for how upset he must have been. But it didn't make any difference. Good reason or not, he'd hurt me, and I wasn't interested in being the one to stick my neck out again.

I let the days pass by, knowing they were weeks for him. I hoped he missed me. But I told myself that I didn't care if he did.

Saturday morning found me sitting on the back porch, having been kicked out of the kitchen by an exasperated Lily. I'd managed to wear down her general good nature until she actually threw a measuring cup at my head and yelled at me to leave. I regretted snapping at her. It wasn't her fault. But that's the thing about sisters, sometimes you can't help but be a little cruel when you're upset. You know they'll have to love you anyway.

The irony wasn't lost on me, but I'd go in and apologize to her in a few minutes. Because apologizing is what you did when you hurt someone you cared about.

I glared in the direction of the forest, willing Leith to feel my evil eye through the Rose Gate. It didn't seem to have any effect, so I sighed and laid back on the sun-warmed planks of the porch. This wasn't helping anything. I needed to either forgive him or get on with my life without him. Constant rage was too exhausting.

I'd just pulled myself back up to go inside and apologize to Lily when I caught sight of a large dark shadow in the forest. A giant, one-eyed grizzly bear lumbered out of the forest edge and sat down in the waist-high ferns.

Leith.

I glanced back at the house, suddenly sure that some-one would catch me talking to a grizzly bear, but all the windows were empty, Amber's black-out blinds firmly in place. With purposeful slowness, I eased to my feet and walked to him, dry grass poking my bare feet. I stopped in front of him and put my hands on my hips.

"Hello, Bear, what do you have to say for yourself?"

The bear hung his head before gently headbutting my shoulder, nearly knocking me over.

"I'll consider it," I told him solemnly.

He just looked at me. Have you ever seen a sorrowful grizzly bear? Let me tell you, they're hard to stay mad at.

"Fine, fine. I'll come to the castle and allow you to apologize properly to me."

He snuffed, and I laughed.

"I need to take care of something inside first. You should probably get back into the forest before Lily calls the conservation officer. I'll meet you on the path in a minute," I told Leith, absently running my hand through the fur on his back before I caught myself. "Sorry." I snatched my hand back.

He gave me his best amused bear look, heaved him-self up, and lumbered his way back into the forest.

After making my apologies and excuses to Lily, I ran into the forest, flip-flops smacking, pilfered pancakes in hand. I met up with Leith on the ATV trail and tossed him a raspberry pancake, which he neatly caught with a single chomp. We took our time hiking up to the miner's cabin. I liked walking with Leith in my forest, even if he was too furry to chat with. Sometimes the time I spent at Kilinaire felt like a dream. It was good to see him here and remember that this was truly my life, not a fantasy.

Soon enough, however, we stepped through the Rose Gate and the late summer smells of sunny pine needles were replaced with the heady scent of the entire castle rose garden in bloom. The roses on the arch seemed to nod happily in the breeze, content now in the company of an exuberant amount of roses in all colors and sizes. I could see the window of my old room surrounded by pink blooms again.

I closed my eyes to breathe it all in, but I was pulled from my reverie by two hands taking mine. I opened my eyes to see Leith, all in black with his eye patch firmly in place. He needed a haircut already.

"You must believe me when I tell you how much I regret my behavior when you visited last," he said. "That day is…difficult for me."

"Ena told me," I said gently.

"Still, I'm sorry for growling at you." He ran his thumb lightly over the back of my hand, and I fought a shiver.

"I did think we were past the growling." I tried to focus on my annoyance with him. It was difficult with the hand rubbing. "Friends shouldn't growl at friends."

"It's true," he agreed solemnly. "And I don't have so many friends that I can afford to growl at them." He hesitated, clearly trying to decide something before continuing. "I do, however, have one other friend I'd like you to meet. If you'd like."

"Of course." A friend? Intriguing.

"Do you truly forgive me, *Àlainn*?"

I was caught by the vulnerability in his voice.

"Truly, Bear. Now introduce me to this friend of yours."

"So…important phone call, then?" I asked Leith as he checked a rather complicated-looking golden pocket watch for the fifth time.

The prince was pacing around the alcove in the library that held the mirror. The first time he pulled it out, the watch had been tangled with a sapphire necklace. Had he been carrying Neala's necklace around ever since I threw it at his head that first evening at Kilinaire? I smiled. It was hard to believe that I had found the prince so intimidating then. "If you're so anxious about the time, weren't you worried you'd lose track of Faerie time going to fetch me?"

"I don't." He flipped the watch closed and motioned me over to the golden bowl.

"You don't worry? Truthfully now."

"I don't lose track."

Before I could ask him what exactly that meant, the water rippled as though someone had dropped a pebble into its center. I leaned in on my tiptoes to see as the water cleared. Leith nudged me with his elbow, and I turned to see him holding three enormous leather-bound books.

"A little light reading?" I eyed the stack. It was easily twelve inches tall.

He set the books down by my feet with a thud. "For you."

"Oh, very funny. It's not my fault that I'm short."

"Who's funny? Who's short?" came a voice from the mirror, startling me enough to make me hop up on the books and stare into the dark water. Sadly, I had to admit it was easier to see from up here.

The watery mirror showed the face of a high fae man. Fair-skinned with freckles to match his perfectly styled, short copper hair, the man's striking features were only surpassed by my memory of Leith from the painting. Still, quite handsome. And looking quite stunned to find me staring back at him.

The man let out a whistle. "Are you going to introduce us, Leith, or should I guess her identity? Tell me about yourself, fair maiden. Are you a rabbit that got turned into a fae, rather than the other way around? An enchantress? A very lost selkie?"

I found myself at a loss for words.

"Tiernan, this is Isobel. Isobel, Tiernan," said Leith.

"Prince Tiernan, actually," pointed out the man. "I mean, High Prince Tiernan, if you want to get technical."

"Yes," sighed Leith. "This is the heir to the Seelie throne and the future ruler of our kingdom, heaven help us."

Tiernan put his hand to his heart in mock pain. "I am wounded by your lack of confidence. Fair lady, please grant me a smile to heal my injured..."

"Ego?" I supplied.

"I see why you like her." Tiernan cocked an elegant copper eyebrow at Leith. "She's a match for you in cruelness."

Leith rolled his good eye at his friend.

"What makes you think he likes me?" I asked, curious.

"Because you're here," the high prince answered simply. "Which is, frankly, very interesting."

"Why is it interesting?"

"Other than the fact that no one has visited Kilinaire in a hundred years, which is interesting in itself, I suppose..."

232

"That's enough, Tiernan," cut in Leith. "I'm sure you don't have much time. What did you need to speak to me about?"

Tiernan gave me a pointed look, and Leith put his hand on my shoulder. "It's fine. Isobel can be trusted. Besides, it's not as if she can go wandering around the faerie countryside telling stories."

"Fine, fine. I was hoping you might have found an answer to my problem, somewhere in all those books of yours."

"Are you under a curse as well?" I asked. Was this the in thing for fae princes?

Tiernan laughed loudly. "A curse? I suppose you could call him that. My father, King Fiachra… It's a long story, but I am running out of time here. Leith, have you found any precedent for breaking the vow?"

Leith sighed. "None that leaves you still in line for the throne."

"You're sure?"

"A deathbed vow is too powerful. I haven't found even one instance where someone has gotten out of one without severe consequences. Your mother bound you both when you and the King agreed to this as she died. Fiachra must pass the crown to you on your two hundredth birthday, and you have to be married to accept it. And as I've shown, even breaking a smaller vow opens you up to too much danger. I can't imagine what Fiachra would twist out of the power released from your breaking that vow to your mother. The best you can do is look at the exact wording and find another way to fulfill it. But I'm not sure it's possible."

"Is getting married really so bad?" I asked, honestly curious. "No nice faerie princesses available?"

Tiernan lost his good humor. He ran his hand over his short hair. "The King is determined to choose a bride for me who is firmly under his influence. Anyone else I've shown interest in has either been frightened off, or, in a couple of cases, met with accidents."

I shivered, remembering what Leith had said about his parents' hunting accident.

"Exactly. Well, Leith, if you think of anything, let me know. I'm getting desperate over here. I know he's planning something for my birthday, but he won't tell me what it is. I'd better go now before anyone notices the mirror spell."

"Wait!" I called out to Tiernan before he broke the connection.

He paused and cocked an eyebrow at me.

"How did you know when to call? I mean, how do you two set up your meetings? Mirror voicemail?"

Tiernan gave Leith a look. Leith shrugged. "I have no idea what she's talking about half the time."

Tiernan sighed. "Here's how it works, lovely girl. I send Leith a message with the date and time of our meeting."

"How?" I pressed.

He mimed a flying bird with his long, pale hands.

I turned to Leith, puzzled. "I thought only the court rulers had the power to use birds like that."

"So, if you do happen to find yourself tripping about the faerie countryside at any point, maybe don't mention that to my father." Tiernan gave a wink and tapped the water on his side. When the ripple cleared, the basin showed empty darkness again.

Leith sighed and paced across the library, obviously on a mission. I was about to join him when the mirror rippled, and the high prince's face appeared in it again.

"Isobel," he whispered urgently, "I'm not sure what Leith has told you about the curse, but knowing him, I'm guessing not that much. You should know there are only two ways Leith's curse can be broken. The first is to kill the curse's originator."

"Moriath," I said.

"Which, as you can guess, is not the safest plan. The other way is to supersede her claim with a stronger one."

"What do you mean?" I asked.

"That's enough, Tiernan." Leith was striding back across the library toward the mirror.

"What I mean, Isobel, is how much do you truly care about my friend?" He opened his mouth to say more, but Leith smacked the water, breaking the connection.

I whirled on Leith, unsteadily keeping my perch on the stack of books to maintain whatever advantage of height it gave me.

"Is there another way to break the curse?" I poked him in the chest with an accusing finger. "What are you not telling me?"

"Isobel." He caught my hand with his wet fingers. "Do you trust me?"

I narrowed my eyes at him. "Of course I do, with my life. But I'm not sure I trust you with your own. Tell me you're not risking it when there's another way to save Kilinaire."

"Tiernan doesn't understand the situation. I've told you. The curse will only be broken when the Unseelie Queen dies."

I glared at him as he helped me down off my stack of books. If he wouldn't tell me, I'd harass someone else until I figured it out.

CHAPTER 27

COME TO THINK OF IT, I'M NOT sure why I thought Miss Chloe would be more helpful than the surly bear was. In fact, she was a little surly herself today.

""I told you, I've given you everything you need." She handed me a stack of picture books. We were setting up for the last week of reading club. One week of Irish fairy tales and then the little ones would be back in school, I would be off to university, and Leith would be what? A bear enslaved to an evil queen? Dead?

"You haven't! And I'm running out of time." I couldn't keep my frustration out of my voice today.

"Frankly, you aren't my only problem right now." She turned to open the doors and let the children into the classroom.

"What is that supposed to mean?!" I wailed.

"It means I'm a very busy faerie godmother right now. Not to mention the year-end party we have yet to plan for next week."

Small humans started pouring into the classroom. I sighed and helped one of the littlest girls who was trying to carry a stack of books that probably outweighed her.

"Oh, Isobel, there is one thing."

I glanced at the faerie who was being swarmed by children. "The sapphire necklace ought to be enough."

"Enough for what?"

"The debt. Don't worry about it right now. Just remember the necklace when you need it. Hello, Charlie. How's your lizard doing?"

And with that I lost her to her flood of tiny adoring fans.

I spent the morning only half aware of what I was doing, going through the motions of helping little hands with glue and scissors while my mind turned through endless circles, trying to solve a problem I still felt utterly unequipped to handle. Leith needed a warrior to help him defeat the Unseelie Queen. Or a magician of skill and power. Maybe a scholar of faerie lore and history. Not an eighteen-year-old girl who liked to read vampire novels.

"Then what happened, Miss Isobel?" asked the freckled little girl at my feet. I pulled my brain back to my current task. I was reading The Frog Prince to the kids today. The Disney version, which hardly even counted as a fairy tale in my book, but the kids liked it.

"Then she kissed the prince, and it broke the evil spell." The little girls cooed and the boys made puking noises. But I just stared at the sparkly illustration of the couple kissing. "Surely not," I murmured. "That would be ridiculous."

Had I been looking in the wrong books for answers? When your curse involved princes, castles, and faerie godmothers, could there be any cure but a kiss?

"And did they live happily ever after?" asked Freckles earnestly.

"Of course they did," I said more firmly. "Because after all, it was true love." Charlie fell over in a fit of disgust. But all I could think of was Prince Tiernan asking me how much I truly cared about his friend. Did I love him? As soon as I asked myself, I knew I did. When had he become more than a friend to me? The thought of losing him when the counter-curse ran out made my blood run cold. I wanted nothing more than a future of happiness for Leith, preferably one that included me in it. But would that be enough to break the spell?

After two days of futile plotting and even an evening spent googling embarrassing things like, *How to know if a*

guy loves you and *How to kiss someone for the first time without being awkward*, I had to admit I needed help. I'd dated a total of two boys in my life and managed to break up with both of them before there was any kissing involved. Clearly, I wasn't an expert in matters of love.

"So, Amber..." I sat down on her bed and tugged an earbud out of her ear. "Can you help me with something?"

"I'm not peeling potatoes or whatever," grumbled Amber, snatching back her earbud. "I'm busy."

"Really." I peeked at her phone where a pink-haired girl was applying stripes of brown makeup to her nose. "What even is this?"

"It's contouring, Bel, to make your nose look narrower. And don't act like you suddenly care about your appearance when clearly you have no one to impress." She gave me a disdainful once-over. From anyone else I would be offended, but this was Amber, and besides, this was why I needed her.

"Actually," I examined my fingernails, "that's what I wanted your help with. You see, there's this guy..."

"What!? You have a boyfriend?" Amber ripped out her headphones and tossed her phone across her bed. "That's amazing! I thought you'd probably die old and alone...with only your books for company."

"Thanks, Amber. That's incredibly sweet of you."

"Maybe some cats," she added helpfully.

"You have a boyfriend?" Lily leaned into the room.

"Let's tell the whole world," I groused.

"I highly doubt anyone else cares about your nerdy love life, Bel," said Amber. I resisted the urge to smack her upside the head. In love.

"Who is it?" asked Lily. "When can we meet him? We need details."

I tried to imagine bringing a grizzly bear home to meet my family. Would Lily feed him cookies?

"You can't meet him yet. He's not actually my boyfriend. I'm not actually sure he, you know, likes me. I mean, he likes me, but..."

"You're adorably pathetic when you babble, but let's get to the point here. Has he kissed you?"

"Well, no, and that's what I'm trying to figure out how to make happen."

"Geez, just kiss him. It's not rocket science! I'm so going to have to support both of you in your old age..."

"Don't worry about me." Lily sat down cross-legged on the bed with us. "Also, what is this? The Victorian era? You need a husband to survive?"

"Wait, you have a boyfriend?" Amber turned on Lily. "Who even are you people, and what have you done with my nerdy sisters?"

"Of course I do! Tony, he's in pre-med with me. You met him at Thanksgiving."

"Tony, Tony, doesn't ring a bell..."

"You said he was just your friend." I bumped my shoulder against Lily's.

"And he was. At first." She smiled at me. "But what about you? Amber's right, you could kiss him. Or better yet, talk to him about it."

"I highly doubt that's better, but yes, talking is also an option," agreed Amber.

"Hmm…" They weren't wrong, but I couldn't help but feel that more would be needed. Surely the spell wouldn't be broken with a "define the relationship" talk. "I want it to be more…"

"Special?" asked Lily.

"Exactly," I said, gratefully. "I want to surprise him with a special date. And I wanted your help."

"You're trying to seduce him!" crowed Amber happily.

"What? No! I just wanted to borrow a dress. I didn't bring anything that nice when we moved, but I know you have a ton. Is there anything that would fit me?"

"Well, it's a good thing we didn't all use our shipping space for five million books when we left Vancouver." Amber bounced up and opened her closet and was greeted by a near-avalanche of clothes. "I'm sure we can find you something."

After what felt like days of trying on clothes, we finally found something. Most of her wardrobe was far too flashy for me. But this last dress was…

"Pretty good," admitted Amber at last.

"It looks fantastic on you," said Lily from the pile of chiffon and sequins on the bed. "Why do you have it, Amber? I've never seen you wear it."

"Oh, it was one of my options for prom, but then we moved out to this hick town where prom is only for grade twelve. Yet another sign that we now live beyond the edge of civilization."

The dress was incredible. Strapless with a fitted bodice and a full skirt fit for a fairy tale princess, all in an airy silk that shifted between rose gold and blush pink, depending on the light. I adored it.

There was just one little problem.

"I can't really breathe," I gasped. And then promptly tripped on the hem. Okay, two problems.

"If you would cut carbs like I said..." Amber helped me back onto my feet.

"I would then also grow two inches? It's so unfair that you're taller than me." I looked regretfully in the mirror. I loved this dress. If I took it back to Kilinaire, I'm sure Deirdre and her army of sewing mice—or so I envisioned them—would be able to alter it for me, but I didn't want to try and sneak a giant bag of tulle and silk past Leith. It would be hard to explain. "I don't think this is going to work."

"Oh, don't be silly." Amber unzipped the back of the dress. Sweet, sweet oxygen. "I know a girl for this."

CHAPTER 28

"I CAN DO IT, BUT IT'LL TAKE a week." The slim, Asian girl turned the dress inside out and eyed the seams critically. She had already measured me—which was awkward—and watched me try on the dress—which was even more awkward.

"You've got four days," said Amber.

"What is this, Project Runway?" The girl glanced up from the dress to glare at Amber. "I said it would take a week and it will take a week! Look at all the alterations I have to do already, and I have to finish up a wedding dress by Friday." She gestured at the pile of clothes on the table behind her. How Amber knew that the local bridal shop did alterations was beyond me, but it did explain why all her clothes fit so perfectly.

"A week is fine…" I tried to remember her name.

"Ella," she said with a sigh.

"What if we pay you double?" Amber persisted.

"Then my stepmother will have twice as much money, and it will still take a week." Ella twisted her long black hair up into a knot and stabbed a blue pencil through it to keep it in place. "Now get out of here, Amber, and don't come back until next Wednesday."

"Thanks so much!" I called as we left the bridal shop, but Ella was already back to her sewing machine.

"Well, I'm sorry. I didn't think it would take so long," groused Amber as we walked back home. "And you know, I've never seen her smile? Not even at school. What that girl needs is a little more fun in her life."

I shuddered to think of what kind of trouble Amber could pull the teenage seamstress into in the name of *fun*.

"It's okay. A week isn't that long." I had continued plotting my perfect romantic set-up, and I needed a chance to visit Kilinaire again and ask Ena for help with a couple of things.

"At least it gives us time to come up with a plan for your hair and makeup," said Amber, cheering up.

"Just promise me, Amber. No nose contouring."

The week flew by. I visited Kilinaire twice, and while Leith was happy to see me, he didn't seem to notice how awkward I was feeling around him. The combination of my realization of my feelings for him and my worry about the curse made me unable to hold up my end of our usual banter. As for the prince, he was almost overly cheerful, preoccupied with pretending to not be worried about the fact that the safe bubble around the castle had shrunk right up to the back door of the castle, cutting them off from the orchards and gardens. The castle residents were living off their stores and meat hunted by Leith and Geanan in animal form. And still the blurry walls of air kept pressing closer and closer. Time was running out for my friends.

The day I had chosen with Ena to put my plan into motion came, and I found myself watching the magic rose like a clock all morning, sneaking peeks into my bag at it during the reading club. I was hoping I had accurately guessed the days passing in Faerie while I slept. I didn't want to be late. After work, I picked up my dress from Ella, who seemed to have some sort of magic of her own because it fit perfectly.

Then Amber did my hair, arranging curls behind a blush pink ribbon that matched my dress. I missed my magical hairdresser as Amber wielded more pins and hair spray than I would have thought possible for a "soft and romantic updo." But if I wanted to surprise Leith, I needed to get ready at home.

"Amber?" I had my eyes closed as she carefully applied who-knows-what with what looked like a paint palette and about twenty brushes.

"Hmmm?" she said around the paintbrush sticking out the side of her mouth.

"Thank you for helping me with this stuff. I've never been as good at it as you and..." I trailed off awkwardly. Amber and I didn't talk about this. Not ever.

"And Mom?" she finished flatly. "You can open your eyes now. I'm done with them."

"Do you miss her?" I asked softly. Of all of us, Amber had been the closest to Mom. Her shopping buddy, her tanning buddy, her gossip buddy. Where I had avoided Mom's parties and bustle, Amber had reveled in them.

"I did at first. Go like this..." Amber made a face, opening her lips slightly. I mimicked her, and she started on my lips. "I hated Dad for driving her away. He knew what she was like, that she loved nice things. He should have kept things together, you know? To keep her happy."

I nodded and she stilled the movement with her hand under my chin.

"No moving." She switched to yet another brush with another color of lip-something. "Then after a while, I hated Mom. How could she tell me I was her favorite person in the world, that I was just like her, that we could practically be sisters, and then up and leave me like that?"

"And now?"

"Now," Amber stopped applying the makeup and looked me in the eye. "Now, I just don't want to turn out like her. And sometimes I'm scared that it's too late. I know I can be such an..."

"Entitled brat?" I suggested teasingly.

"Sure, that." She huffed out a laugh, and reached for a pot of gold glitter. "What if that's all there is to me?"

"Hey." I held her hand. "It's not. It's never too late to decide who you want to be. And you've got me and Lily. You know that."

"I know, I know," she said briskly, blinking back tears. "Now close your eyes again."

"Wait!" I was suddenly alarmed as I clued into what she was holding. "No glitter!"

"Oops, too late." Amber gave a careless laugh and blew fine gold dust all over me.

"Are you ready for your dress yet?" I could see Lily in the mirror, standing at the doorway unzipping the garment bag.

"Lily, please tell me that I don't look like a manic sparkly unicorn," I pleaded, turning in my chair. Amber beamed beside me.

"No, Bel." Lily came over to smooth a nonexistent stray hair. "You look beautiful."

I heard Dad tromp into the house as my sisters helped me into the dress. The phone rang, and we all paused, but we couldn't make out his conversation. I checked the mirror one last time to ensure Lily was telling the truth. She was. Amber knew her stuff. Hopefully, I wouldn't be finding gold glitter in my hair for the next month. I grabbed my bag, slipped on my ballet flats, and headed for the stairs, my sisters after me.

"You're looking awfully short," said Amber. "Where are those killer heels I picked out for you?"

"Killer is the right word for them." I stopped on the step and lifted the hem of my dress enough to show her the dark leather flats I had taken from Kilinaire. "The heels are in my bag. Don't worry, I'll put them on when I get there."

"Those are really cute." Amber bent down to examine my shoes. "Where'd you buy them?"

"Um." I couldn't very well tell her that they'd been custom-made by a leipreachán cursed to look like a badger.

"Where are you going?" called Dad from the living room, saving me from replying.

I paused in the doorway. "Out. I won't be late."

"Not tonight," he said shortly and turned back to the TV. "No one's going out tonight."

"Now he decides to be overprotective?" whispered Amber from behind me. "It's a little late for him to suddenly take up parenting."

"I can't stay home," I hissed back, resisting the urge to check the rose again. I wanted to be there for dusk, Kilinaire time, and I didn't have time for this.

"Distract him, Amber," ordered Lily under her breath. "Bel can sneak out the back door."

"Everyone is so rebellious tonight," Amber whispered happily. "I love it!" She ran to the kitchen and grabbed a can of Dad's beer from the fridge before sauntering into the living room.

"What are you doing with my beer? You get a job to pay for that?" Dad took a sullen swig from his third can, judging by the empties on the coffee table.

"I'm pre-gaming," she explained reasonably, cracking it open. "I'm going to a party in an hour, and really, bush parties aren't enough fun to arrive sober, you know?"

"Should we be more concerned about her?" I whispered to Lily.

"I'll deal with her tonight. You worry about her later. This is your night, now get out of here," said Lily, waving me toward the back door.

"Okay, okay. Love you." I hugged her quickly and dashed out the back door, closing it more gently than necessary, given the amount of yelling being emitted from the living room.

I stood at the entrance to the Rose Gate, watching my rose as it barely began to curl in on itself before I stepped through. Late afternoon heat disappeared into dusky coolness as Kilinaire's rose garden appeared around me. He was there, waiting in his dark formal wear like he would always wear to dinner, kept from being too perfect by the scars and eye patch that I was starting to love.

"*Àlainn*," said Leith huskily, taking in my sparkling appearance. "What are you up to?"

I willed the butterflies in my stomach to still and took his outstretched hand. "Happy birthday, Bear."

CHAPTER 29

"HOW DID YOU KNOW?" Leith asked, wonder in his eyes as he brushed a carefully placed curl back from my face. I couldn't help the shiver that ran up my spine.

"Oh, you know, I have my magical ways, too."

He just gave me a look.

"Well, the magic of female gossip, which is a powerful thing all its own." I gave him a wink. "I figured out the date from Miss Chloe and lined up the exact day with Ena. Although neither of them would tell me exactly how old you're turning today. Apparently, you aren't much of a party guy."

"Not generally, no." He gave a smile.

"Well, this year you're getting one. Come with me." I grabbed his hand and led him through the dusky garden to my favorite bench in the hedge maze. Even in the fading light, it was obvious the protective bubble around the castle was growing dangerously small. I wasn't sure there was anything left of the side gardens, and even the back tower was hard to make out. Had part of the castle itself been lost? Panic threatened to rise up in me, but I pushed it down firmly. No need for panic. I had a plan.

"You sit here." I pointed at the end of the bench. He obliged. "And close your eyes."

He gave a sigh of long-suffering and did as I said.

I pulled out the little box from my bag, setting it in front of him on the bench. His lashes fluttered, but I hissed at him. He squeezed them shut again. After lifting out the chocolate cupcake I had carefully brought in a pastry box from Pie in the Sky, I pulled a lighter from my purse and fumbled a couple times before lighting the striped candle in the middle.

"Okay, you can look."

He smiled at the cupcake, picking it up to examine the candle.

"Traditionally you'd have a candle for each year of your life, but even if I knew how many to bring, I have a feeling the cake would be a fire hazard. So, this is what you get."

He gave me a rare laugh in response, making me glow inside like the little candle.

"You need to make a wish, a birthday wish, and blow it out."

"What sort of thing do people wish for?"

"I have no idea. If you say it out loud, the wish doesn't come true."

He gazed at me steadily and blew out the dancing flame, then pulled the candle out and broke the cupcake in two, handing half to me. It was delicious. I bet everything Neve baked was delicious.

After we licked our fingers clean, I rummaged around in my purse again, finding my phone.

"And what's this?"

"This," I said smugly, "is my own magic." I pulled out a portable speaker—also Amber's. I'm more of a headphones girl—and clicked over to my music app. Swelling notes of stringed instruments filled the air.

Leith's eyes widened. "Magic indeed! It almost seems familiar. It's not faerie music, is it?"

"Tchaikovsky, actually. I'm fresh out of faerie music. But I do have one more bit of magic up my sleeves, figuratively," I added as he teasingly ran a finger down my bare arm. I could tell myself the goosebumps down my arms were from the coolness of the evening, but that would be a lie. I batted his hand away. "I need to concentrate."

I closed my eyes and felt for the magic all around me. I could feel the Rose Gate and the pulsing glow of various magics at work in the castle. The tiny pricks of magic in the garden danced around us like motes of dust, as magic does in Faerie. I could even feel the slow beat of magic through my heart, my own energy. But I ignored all of those and focused on the small bits of potential I could feel threaded all around the garden. Ena had taken care of her part of the preparations.

"Light up," I ordered the little magical specks.

I opened my eyes to an enchanted garden. It was even more beautiful than I'd imagined, with little golden lights sparkling in the hedges and rose bushes, draped from the trees and topiaries, and lazily drifting in the fountains. The rose garden felt like a reflection of the sky where the stars were now coming out.

"So." Leith rose from the bench. "Here I am with a beautiful girl, music, and Sheerie lights. There's only one thing to do now." Taking my hand, he pulled me up into his arms. I took an unsteady breath.

"Dance with me?"

"Sure," I answered with false casualness, and we were off.

"I've never been much good at dancing," I admitted as we swirled around the fountain and out through the maze of hedges. His hand was hot against my back while I tried not to trip in my stupid shoes. "Okay, to be honest, I haven't really tried, apart from what they made us learn in school. But you seem to know what you're doing. Not bad for a proclaimed hater of parties and court life."

"My mother taught me." He twirled me out in a satisfying swirl of silk skirt. "When I was young. All I wanted to do was train to be a great warrior with the Fianna, but she convinced me dancing would help me with my sword work."

I laughed at his tone, imagining what it must have been like to raise a grumpy little Leith. "And did it?"

"I'm not sure she had any evidence it would. I think she just wanted to make me less embarrassing at court. But I can dance well, and I can fight well, so perhaps there was something to it after all."

"I'm grateful to her for that. You dance well enough for both of us." I'm sure my dancing still wouldn't impress my high school gym teacher, let alone the faeries of the Seelie Court, but with Leith's guiding hand on my back, I could pretend I was graceful and elegant.

The song rose around us, and I laughed as he spun me out once more. I missed my footing as I twirled back in, and he caught me against him. We stopped dancing, and the music seemed to fade into the distance. Suddenly, nothing existed in the world beyond the two of us.

Now's your chance! My brain clamored, but the rest of me froze. Wait, what was I thinking? Trying to engineer True Love's Kiss? I loved Leith. I mean, I was pretty sure I did, but I didn't even know if he felt anything beyond friendship for me.

I was jolted out of my chaotic thoughts by his hand grazing the back of my neck and his eyes dropping to my mouth. I started to say something, confess to my plotting maybe, but nothing came out as he gently pulled me toward him and tipped up my chin, brushing my lips with his.

Oh. That.

But he stopped too soon, looking down at me solemnly. "*Àlainn*." He sounded like he might apologize. "I..."

But that's as far as I let him get. I reached up and pulled him down to me, kissing him back in a way that left no room for apologies. My eyes closed, and I forgot everything but the feeling of him against me and the whisper of his lips on mine.

When at last he pulled back, I stood with my eyes closed, waiting for my pounding heart to slow back down.

Surely that had been a kiss of true love. I knew my heart would never be the same, and it seemed impossible that a kiss like that could exist in the world and not contain magic.

But when I opened my eyes, impossibly, the world was unchanged. Even in the dim light of stars and twinkling lights, it was clear that the bubble around the castle remained. The back tower was still gone. No cries of happiness came from transformed faeries within the castle.

The curse wasn't broken.

I had failed.

"Isobel." The prince peered into my eyes, and I tried to smile, but I couldn't keep the devastation I was feeling inside from showing on my face. "What's wrong?"

Clearly this wasn't how you were supposed to feel after a kiss like that. I tried to explain. "I thought that...the curse..." I trailed off as his expression changed from one of concern as he understood what I'd been trying to do tonight.

Raw pain flicked in his gaze. I had so badly wanted him to let me in, and when he finally opened up, I fumbled it.

"This was just another one of your ideas, wasn't it? The salt and the sage didn't work, so you'd try one more thing?" I could see his walls going back up as his hurt expression turned steely.

I opened my mouth and then closed it again. He wasn't wrong, but he didn't understand.

"I thought..." He looked down, running a hand through his hair. "Obviously I am still a fool. Tiernan always said I was naive when it came to women, and twice now I've proved him right." He took a steadying breath and met my eyes again, his gaze stony. "You've had your fun, a summer playing with magic and curses, but I think you should leave now."

"No, Leith, you don't understand!" Something broke inside me at the look on his face. He couldn't truly be comparing me to the Unseelie Queen. "This wasn't a game! I was only trying to..."

"Break the curse, I know." The music continued to play around us, sounding mockingly happy as my world crumbled. "Be the hero. Like one of your story books."

"Leith," I pleaded, "please listen to me. I didn't mean to hurt you. That kiss was real."

"You didn't plan all this? A perfectly romantic evening to manipulate me into kissing you? Like the happy ending of some tale?"

I had no answer for him. Because, of course, I had.

He held my arm, not as gently as before, and all my borrowed gracefulness left as he steered me toward the Rose Gate.

"I'm sorry," I bit back my tears. We were almost at the Rose Gate now. "But, Bear…"

He spun me to look at him and waited, bristling with impatience.

I love you.

But the words withered inside me under the heat of his glare.

"I think it would be best if you don't come back to Kilinaire." With that he released my arm, sending me stumbling back through the Rose Gate.

My dress tangled on the thorns of the roses as the heat of late afternoon greeted me. I spun around, determined to go back through and find the words to make him understand. But when I stepped through the arch of tightly closed dark red roses, I only entered the meadow with the miner's cabin slowly rotting in front of me. I walked around and tried again. Nothing. I tried ten more times before I collapsed onto the ground in tears, my dress settling like a cloud around me.

He'd closed the gate against me. There was no going back this time.

I had lost him.

CHAPTER 30

I DON'T KNOW HOW LONG I sat there in the forest. I'm not usually much for crying, but I found that I couldn't stop. I was equal parts remorseful and angry. I felt like such a child in my princess dress playing like my life was a fairytale, when it was obviously anything but. I should have just talked to Leith and told him how I felt. Yes, that would have been terrifying, but this...this was so much worse.

But on the other hand, how could he kiss me like that, like I was the most precious thing in the world, and then throw me out a minute later?

I wanted to sustain a good, bitter rage. But I just hurt too much. Eventually, I noticed that the sun was close to the top of the mountain. Dusk came earlier in late August, and I had no desire to run into those wolves again. I picked myself up and rubbed my eyes with the back of my hands. Amber was going to kill me when she saw what I had done to her careful makeup job. I looked around, feeling like I'd forgotten something. Dang it, my bag was back in the garden. So much for my favorite shoes. I sighed shakily and pulled off my sparkling high heels before starting for home.

When I reached our back yard, I stopped at the edge of the forest. Something felt wrong.

Our back door was wide open, hanging on only half its hinges. I broke into a run. A pane of glass in Amber's window was broken. Hesitating on the back steps, I listened for a few seconds, but the house was silent. I crept into the house, wincing as the old wood floor creaked under my steps. I stepped around broken plates and overturned kitchen chairs. A groan came from the living room. I rushed in, avoiding shards of glass with my bare feet. My father moaned on the floor by the broken coffee table, his leg twisted in a nasty break. He was bleeding from his forehead and covered in bruises.

"Dad!" I ran over and checked him over briefly. He didn't seem to be bleeding badly, but I didn't know much about first aid. "Hold still. I'm going to call 911."

His eyes fluttered as he tried to rally himself to speak, but I shushed him and ran to use the phone in the hallway. The operator assured me that both the ambulance and the police were on their way and warned me not to move him. Coming back into the living room,

I found the afghan that was usually on our couch in a corner and gently covered my dad with it.

"Bel," he said hoarsely, "your sisters…"

"Where are they?" I asked in a panic. I should have checked upstairs. What if they were hurt or worse? My brain refused to go there.

"They're gone, Bel. I'm so sorry." Tears leaked out of the corners of his eyes. "You need to get out of here."

"What do you mean gone?" My stomach turned to ice.

"They took them. You have to run, Bel, before those men come back."

"You're not making any sense, Dad. Who took them? What men? I'm not going anywhere until the ambulance gets here."

"Your mother." He winced. "Oh, how I loved her. From the first time I saw her. She was so beautiful. You're looking more and more like her as you get older…" He trailed off, his eyes closing.

"Dad! Stay with me here." What was he talking about Mom for? Did he have a concussion?

His eyes opened again, with effort. "But you know your mother, she needed a certain lifestyle. She deserved everything I could give her, but then…"

"Then what?" I asked, warily.

"I lost the business. The shareholders bullied me out in the end. Those vultures. I built that company up from nothing. I didn't have anything left to make another start. You have to understand, Bel, she was going to leave me."

"She did leave you."

"This was two years ago. I tried to borrow money everywhere, and then she approached me."

"She?" A sudden chill ran down my spine. "Who, Dad?"

"She never told me her name. She always had a dog with her. Big wolf of a thing. And, she was beautiful, but cold, you know? Not like your mother. But she lent me the money."

"What did you do, Dad?" I was growing more terrified by the second.

"Three times she gave me money, but I couldn't make it work again. I couldn't get any investors to trust me. And your mother, she was never willing to settle for a simpler life. She shouldn't have had to."

I could hear sirens distantly now. I went to look out the window.

"She promised to collect my collateral, but when we moved out here…I thought she would never find us…"

I looked back at him sharply.

"What did you put up for collateral?"

He was silent for so long that I was afraid he'd passed out, but then he said tiredly, "You girls."

I closed my eyes.

"She lent me money three times and each time made me promise that if I was unable to repay her, she would take one of my daughters. You have to understand, Bel, I was so sure I would make the money back. So sure..."

The ambulance was turning down our road now. I gave my dad's shoulder one last pat, suddenly not caring if I ever saw him again. "Goodbye, Dad. I'm going to go find my sisters."

He stiffened, trying to rise but failing. "No, Bel. You have to run as far as you can. There's nothing you can do. The people who took them...I...I'm not even sure they were human."

"Well, then, it's a lucky thing I know a bear."

I left the living room without another look at the broken man who had sold me to the Unseelie Queen.

PART 4

CHAPTER 31

RAN BACK THROUGH THE FOREST IN my bare feet, hiking up my dress. It still caught on bushes and twigs, shredding the hem Ella had spent a week fixing for me. It wasn't the most practical outfit for a rescue.

But, if I had stayed any longer, I would have had to talk to the police, and there was no way I would have gotten out of there in time. It was already growing darker. My mind played back the howls and snarls of Moriath's wolves until I could almost hear them over my pounding heart and panting breath.

I reached the Rose Gate before darkness fell. It might have been only an hour for me since Leith had thrown me out, but maybe enough time had passed in Tír na nÓg for him to be willing to talk to me. I didn't dare hope he would ever forgive me.

I stepped through the Rose Gate and remained in my forest. Apparently, he was still upset.

"Leith!" I yelled, hoping he was paying attention to his mirror. "Leith, please let me in. I need your help."

I walked through again. Nothing.

"Leith! Please, it's getting dark."

The gate remained closed to me. I glared at it ineffectually and then jumped as a furry little body wrapped around my ankle.

"Rani!" I picked her up, and she licked my chin with her rough little tongue. I held her, running my hand over her soft fur. Cats. Ena had said that cats went where they wanted, magic or no magic. Curse or no curse.

I held Rani up to my face for a serious talk. "Can you help me get through the gate?"

She purred in response.

"Is that a yes? All right, I'll take it."

Holding her in my arms, I took a deep breath and closed my eyes before stepping through the gate again. The air grew warmer and the scent of roses grew stronger. Before I even had time to realize it had worked, I was tackled to the ground, Rani jumping out of my arms with an offended yowl.

"Isobel!" said Leith in surprise. I was pinned to the ground underneath him with a silver sword at my throat.

"Um." I swallowed nervously. "I know you're a bit upset with me, but is the sword really necessary?"

"Right, sorry." The prince helped me to my feet and sheathed his sword. "You weren't who I was expecting to come through the gate."

"Who were you planning to greet at sword point?" I grumbled, brushing dirt off my ball gown. It was a lost cause. The dress wasn't going to be making any prom appearances after this mess.

"The Unseelie Queen," replied Leith grimly, and I looked up at him in surprise, then glanced behind him.

I covered my mouth in shock. Kilinaire was gone. Lost behind the barrier as Miss Chloe's counter-curse now only extended to the rose garden. The garden was inhabited by all the castle's residents, camping in tents and shelters between the hedges.

"I sent word to her with one of Tiernan's birds, and I set the gate to let her through, but I don't have the mirror anymore so... I apologize."

"Oh Leith." I took a step toward him, and he took a step back, preserving the distance between us. Not forgiven, then. I felt the loss of him all over again with that one step.

"Isobel." Ena scampered up to us from the hedges. "What are you doing here, my dear?"

I refocused on my reason for coming. "It's Moriath," I told them, and Leith's attention sharpened. "She has my sisters."

"Are you sure?"

"I'm sure. Her men broke into my house, and…and they beat up my Dad and stole my sisters."

"Why would they do something like that? What value would your sisters have to the Unseelie Queen?"

"My father." I took a shaky breath. "He put them up as collateral against a debt with Moriath."

Leith's face became alarmed.

"Us." I amended softly. "He bargained with all three of us, for money to try and keep my mother from leaving."

"How much does he owe her?"

"What?"

"Moriath, how much money did your father borrow from her?"

"I have no idea." I hadn't even thought of that. "Does it matter? Can't we just steal them back?"

"It's not that simple." Leith ran a hand through his hair. "Faerie bargains are binding. If you steal them back, she'll simply come for them again, and she'll have every right to. We have to pay your father's debt if you ever want to bring them home. He gave his vow to Moriath. If you try to break a bargain with the Unseelie Queen, you'll end up…"

"Cursed," I finished. Because, of course, that's what had happened to Leith.

I thought back to the phone calls, but the debt had never been mentioned in more than vague terms, and I certainly hadn't paid enough attention to my parents' finances over the past year to have any idea how much money they had received. I didn't even know if there would be bank records. Not that I had time to go poking around for that sort of thing.

"Wait." I held up my hand. "Miss Chloe said something earlier this week. She said the sapphire necklace would be enough to cover the debt. I had no idea what she was talking about, but she must have meant my father's debt."

Leith blanched. He reached into a pocket inside his long dark coat and pulled out the necklace I had thrown at him that first evening at Kilinaire. Scrolling gold and sparkling blue gems. Neala's necklace. He looked at it for a long moment and then handed it to me.

I didn't know what to say. "But, Leith…"

"No, it's fine. She would want it to be used to save them. I know it."

"But it's not even your debt. I'm sorry that I'm dragging you into this."

"Ah, *Àlainn*, do you think it's a coincidence Moriath put your family in her debt? That she bargained for the right to steal you away and enslave you? I don't think you're the one dragging me into anything. This is yet another cost of my broken vow to her. She's still finding ways to punish me through those I love."

"How would the queen know about me? This was two years ago. I hadn't even met you yet." I went cold at the thought of Moriath targeting me. But had Leith just said he loved me? Probably not the right time to get into that.

"The same way Clíodhna knew the price to free your sisters. Remember when I showed you the mirror?"

"You said a strong magic user could use them to see the past or the future. Moriath can see the future? But that's... How can we fight against someone like that?" I was never going to see my sisters again. How could I outwit someone who knew exactly which trap I would fall into?

"It's not that exact. No one can know the future before it happens. She can see bits and pieces of possible futures and guess from there." He ran his hand through his hair and glanced around at the makeshift camp in the rose garden with a sigh. "We'd better get going."

"But I thought you said Moriath was coming here?" I hugged my arms around me. What was happening to my sisters right now? They must be so frightened.

"I should have known she would never let me have the upper hand like that. She stole your sisters to draw us away from Kilinaire. The Unseelie Queen is choosing where she faces us and what form I'll be in." He fingered the hilt of his sword regretfully. A century of daily training he wouldn't be able to benefit from as a bear.

"So, it's a trap, then," I said flatly.

"Your father said Moriath's men took your sisters. She didn't come herself?"

I shook my head mutely.

"Then our best chance is to find your sisters before they can deliver them to the queen. We'll send the necklace back with one of her men."

"One of her wolves," I corrected. "The sun is nearly down."

"Wolves, then." Leith considered this. "They'll be harder to reason with as wolves. I wish I could check the mirror, but the nearest faerie gate from your forest is in an old gold mine up the mountain from your Rose Gate. That must be where they're planning to meet her."

"I can't go climbing up a mountain like this." I gestured to my torn dress. I turned to Ena, who was still listening by our feet. "I don't suppose you have a more practical dress in one of those tents?"

"I'm afraid not," she said regretfully. "But I do have some scissors."

"Scissors, then. It's not like this dress is worth saving anymore. And then we deal with Moriath." I had a nasty feeling this night was going to cost us more than a necklace.

CHAPTER 32

W E DIDN'T MAKE IT FAR BEFORE THE wolves found us.

We were traveling deeper into the mountains, toward the old gold mine. Leith knew the area from his wanders in bear form, but I had never hiked this far from home. Ena had found me a pair of scissors, and I cut my once gorgeous dress off at midcalf. Leith had produced the bag I had left after his disastrous birthday party, my shoes still in it. I was grateful beyond words to have him here with me, even if I was keenly aware of the space he kept between us.

And so we hiked, the shadows growing deeper as the light faded. I could still see the forest around me, but soon I'd have to rely on Leith's grizzly bear night vision to guide us.

When I heard the first howl in the distance, I froze. The memory of being prey is not something your body forgets. And I had to admit my brain wasn't fully convinced we were fine, either. Leith turned and jerked his head for me to keep moving. Right. I gave my head a shake and followed him again, faster this time, but it was hard going without a trail in the dark, and the wolves quickly gained on us at my stumbling human pace. Leith stopped so suddenly that I crashed into him. He crouched down beside me.

"Seriously?" I hissed, realizing what he was thinking. "Have you ever tried this?"

He snorted in response. The howling came again, closer this time.

"All right, all right." I clambered up onto his wide back and sank my hands into the thick fur of his shoulder hump. "Okay, I'm ready."

He lumbered up to his feet. I gripped as hard as I could with my legs, hoping I wasn't holding on too tight but terrified of falling off. And with good reason. I had ridden horses a few times growing up, but bears don't run anything like a horse does. Leith ate up the ground in bounds, but soon I could hear the wolves again. And then I could see them. Dark shadows darting between the trees. Bright eyes reflecting the moonlight. They were almost upon us.

Leith stopped suddenly, turning and rising up on his hind legs, causing me to tumble to the ground behind him.

Before I could say anything snarky about the lack of warning, he let out a breathy roar. Even knowing he was on my side, the sound sent a shiver through me. The wolves circled us, pacing. I counted only three of them this time. The rest must be up ahead still with my sisters. Even with our improved odds, I was terrified. I scrambled up, pressing my back to Leith's and pulled out the silver dagger he had given me before we left. If only I had taken him up on his offer of further weapons training. As it was, I had to assume that the pointy end went into the wolves. Hopefully the magic it contained would give me the advantage I desperately needed.

And then, through some unknown signal or wolfish instinct, they all attacked. The moon was hidden behind a cloud, and it was almost fully dark, but I did my best to keep behind Leith as they battled. It was terrifying not being able to see what was happening, and I confess I screamed when one suddenly snarled beside me. I threw up my arms as it leaped on me and knocked me to the ground.

I lashed out wildly with my dagger and heard a yelp as it connected with the wolf. I couldn't tell if I'd done much damage. I scrambled to my feet, listening for the creature in the dark, before it came at me again. I cried out as I felt teeth sink into my calf. I couldn't die here, in the dark in the woods. Who would save my sisters if the wolves ate me? Quickly, while I still knew where the wolf was, I pulled myself together and focused all my will on the silver dagger, feeling the magic still inside it.

"Just die already," I ground out before I drove my dagger into the wolf's head. The magic exploded out of the dagger, just like that day in the training arena with Leith. I sobbed with relief as the wolf went limp and slid off me. Thankfully the darkness kept me from seeing what was left of the beast.

When the ringing in my ears lessened, I could hear my hitched breathing, but aside from that, the forest was silent. What had happened with Leith and the other two wolves? I strained my ears into the dark and then yipped as I felt Leith's muzzle nudge my cheek. I leaned into his solid side and then reached into my shoulder bag, rooting around blindly for my phone. Eventually I found it and turned it to flashlight mode to give us a little light.

I shone the light on the leg the wolf had bitten. It didn't look awesome, that was for sure. It didn't hurt as much as I would have thought, and distantly I considered that I might be in shock. Oh well, at least I was alive. I tore another strip off the bottom of my rose gold dress and bound it up as best I could. Prom dresses aren't really made for bandaging.

"Are you hurt?" I asked Leith.

He snuffed in reply.

"Is that an 'I'm awesome' snuff or an 'I'm bleeding out' snuff?" I pulled myself up to my feet, leaning on him to keep the weight off my bad leg.

Trying to do a medical examination on a large and surly grizzly bear in the dark with only a phone for light is exactly as easy as it sounds. He growled lightly at me and shrank back when I reached his left shoulder. I couldn't get a good look, but it was sticky with blood in a few places.

"I'm not sure how to bandage this." I felt helpless. He glared at me out of his good eye, ready to get going again.

"You're sure you're okay?"

He just knelt down in reply. I sighed, but I clearly wasn't running anywhere after that last encounter. Turning off my phone to save the battery, I tucked it back into my bag and climbed up onto his back. I tried to keep from holding on near his injured shoulder as he set off again, this time at a less frantic, although still steady pace.

I was growing tired, but the throbbing of my leg increased as we continued on toward the mine, helping me to stay awake. I supposed the shock was wearing off. If only I had enough magic to heal us both, but here in the human world we would have to struggle along without it.

I strained my ears to listen for my sisters and the other four fae, who would be wolves by now. How terrifying Lily and Amber must be finding this whole thing. I prayed we would catch up with them before they reached the faerie gate.

Suddenly the forest opened up around us. We had reached the old gold mine. The moonlight faintly illuminated abandoned buildings and rusted bits of machinery.

In the side of the mountain, a tunnel seemed to radiate darkness like the mouth of some great devouring beast. And at the opening of the tunnel, I saw my sisters.

They didn't look hurt, but they were being herded into the tunnel by the remaining four wolves. As I watched, Amber balked at the tunnel entrance. She'd never been much for small spaces. The nearest wolf snarled and nipped at her heels.

"I'm going, geez," she snarled back, her voice echoing faintly into the tunnel as she stepped into the inky blackness, Lily holding her hand tightly. One wolf stayed at the entrance, sitting down to keep watch.

"This is all my fault," I whispered, helpless, to Leith. He huffed to tell me I was being ridiculous and quietly made his way to the tunnel entrance, keeping us to the shadows of the buildings and trees as much as he could.

The wolf pricked its ears once or twice but didn't seem to see us. When we reached the shadow of the nearest building, the wolf sniffed the air and trotted our way.

I slid off Leith's back and flattened myself into the wall of the shack, clutching my dagger. We waited at the corner of the building at the very edge of the shadow. A few paces from us, the wolf stopped and sniffed again, then raised its muzzle to howl a warning to its partners.

Before it could make more than a yip, Leith was upon it. It didn't last more than a minute. A lone wolf isn't any match for a male grizzly bear, even an injured one. I winced as it went down with a crunch and stayed down.

Leith motioned me forward with a jerk of his head, and I hobbled to catch up.

With my hand on his good shoulder for balance, we entered the dark mine. I looked back wistfully one last time at the silver light of the clearing and noticed a trail of inky splotches on the ground behind us. A quick pat of my bandage told me the blood wasn't mine. Leith was more badly injured than he was letting on.

Three wolves left, and a faerie gate which was who knew how deep underground. That led to the Unseelie Court.

"I don't suppose you have a plan?" I whispered to Leith.

He snorted in response.

"That's what I was afraid of," I muttered under my breath, almost tripping as he halted in the dark. We had reached a fork in the tunnels. I paused beside him, but I could barely see, and I didn't hear anything beyond an occasional drip in the cool, dank tunnel. I reached out and felt the hewn stone wall, rough and clammy. My fingers found a carving in the rock, and I traced the lines of a strange symbol. It felt different, but something about it made me think of the symbol on the cairn marking the way to the Rose Gate. If only I could see what it was.

Leith started moving again, and then suddenly up ahead a light flashed on, setting off a wave of growls from the wolves. Leith crowded me back a step, and we hid behind the corner, peeking around into the small chamber beyond. The light was Amber, of course. If anyone could be trusted to carry a phone into a faerie kidnapping, it was her.

"Calm down," she told the wolves testily. "I just wanted some light. It's not as if I have a cell signal in the middle of some old mine."

Her light bounced off flecks and ribbons of gold winding around the small, rough chamber they were huddled inside. Behind them I could see the edge of a round doorway carved into the wall. Unlike the tunnel, the doorway was obviously carved with great skill, perfectly circular with intricate swirls in the stone edging it. I could just make out a gold plate bolted to the bottom of the circular doorway. It hummed with magical energy. The other side of the doorway was darkness, but whatever lay there in our world was unimportant because it was, of course, the Unseelie Queen's faerie gate.

I gripped Leith's shoulder. We had to get to my sisters before the wolves activated the gate and took them away. What were they waiting for?

Between one breath and the next, I got my answer.

She stepped through the stone gate into the chamber. The fae queen seemed too large for the small space, her antlered crown nearly scraping the ceiling. Everything about her was cold and pale, from her blue-tinged white hair to the icy light that shone out from the jewels around her neck and dripping onto her forehead. The white furs draped around her seemed more for decoration than protection from the cold.

She fixed her cold gaze on Lily and Amber, and I could feel the power rolling off her. It was like nothing I had felt before. There was none of the normal pleasant humming. The Unseelie Queen's magic made the hair stand up on my arms and set my teeth on edge. I prayed frantically under my breath without even knowing what I said. I was utterly terrified.

The Unseelie Queen had come for my sisters.

CHAPTER 33

"GOOD WORK, BOYS." The wolves crowded around the Unseelie Queen, and she knelt down to give them approving pats and scratches.

A huge fae man stepped through the gate behind her, as dark as the queen was light. He had some sort of pattern shaved into the closely cropped sides of his hair, with long swinging braids down his back, but what held my attention was the casual way he carried his wicked-looking silver axe.

The queen turned to the tall warrior. "Now, Kylian, collect the other two over there, and we'll go home."

I froze, futilely pressing myself against the wall of the tunnel as I heard heavy footsteps on the stone floor coming our way. When I reached in my bag for the silver dagger, it had barely a hum of magic left. I must have used up its stored magic on the wolf.

"Leith, darling," the queen called. "I'm so pleased Bel convinced you to come with her. Thank you for saving me the trouble of traveling to Kilinaire to fetch you."

Leith growled deep in his throat and stepped around the corner into Moriath's light. He was trying his best to shield me, but I could see that he was moving much more slowly now. In the brighter light, the blood I'd suspected earlier was clearly visible, running freely down his front shoulder. From the way he moved and the dark red trail behind him, there must be other injuries as well. We needed to get this sorted out quickly. He was running out of time.

The warrior, Kylian, stopped a few paces away from the injured grizzly, but his expression was more amused than fearful, and I hated him for it.

I took a deep breath and stepped out of the tunnel, moving between Moriath's henchman and my prince, the dagger clenched in my hand.

"Bel!" cried Lily. Tears streaked her face as she clutched Amber's hand. I attempted a reassuring smile at my sisters before turning back to their fae captors.

"I've come to repay my father's debt to you." I ignored the giant man in front of me and addressed the Unseelie Queen, willing my voice to be steady.

"And this must be Bel." Moriath smiled at me, and the smile reminded me of a crocodile. "Your father described you perfectly. You really are a beauty."

I flinched at the reminder of my father's betrayal but reached into my bag with my free hand and felt for the sapphire necklace. I snagged a finger on the thorns of the rose that was still jumbled in with the other things in my bag. A reminder of how happy we'd been, just hours ago.

The necklace hummed softly as I pulled it out, holding it up for Moriath to see. A cold fire sparked in the queen's eyes at the sight of Neala's necklace.

"Are you sure it's wise to bargain with the Queen of the Unseelie Fae?" asked Kylian with a light warning in his deep voice.

"This isn't a bargain," I countered firmly. I turned back to Moriath. "These jewels are enough to repay you and more, I'd guess. The debt is paid. Please let my sisters go."

"Not only beautiful but brave too," Moriath mused, gliding across the rough floor toward me. She motioned her warrior back behind her and plucked the necklace out of my hands. I felt a chill where her fingers brushed mine, like the burn of touching metal on a cold winter's day. "The Sapphires of Airmid," the queen breathed reverently, examining the necklace with interest.

Moriath turned her cold gaze back on me. "This will suffice to pay your father's debt. Regrettably. I did hope to get to know you sweet girls better. If you ever want a place in the Unseelie Court, do let me know."

A shiver ran down my spine. "I don't think so."

"Pity." She gave a liquid shrug. "I'll just have to be content with your prince, then." She said it indifferently, but I could tell by the glint in her eyes that she was baiting me for a reaction. All of this was a game to her, and my sisters and I had never been the prize she was really after.

I heard Leith growl again and risked a glance behind me. He didn't look good. His eye was glassy, and blood still ran down his front leg, pooling under him on the stone floor. He'd spent years working to be strong enough, fast enough to defeat Moriath and free his household from her curse, but in the end, it was out of his hands. Moriath had outmaneuvered him, and his plans had come to nothing. It would be up to me. Even if I didn't see how I could possibly be up to the task, I also couldn't fail him.

I raised my depleted silver dagger and pointed it at the queen. Her guard raised an eyebrow, wisely not seeing me as much of a threat. Still, I willed my hand to be steady, my voice to be firm. "Lily, Amber, get out of here. I'll meet you outside shortly."

"Yes, girls, you're free to go." Moriath didn't so much as glance at them, eyeing me with amusement. "But do be careful in those woods at night. I wouldn't want you to run into any more trouble with wolves."

"I don't think that will be a problem," I told the queen. "There aren't any wolves out there. Not alive anyway."

Her icy mask slipped momentarily as rage flashed in her eyes. It was gone as quickly as it had come, but I knew she hadn't expected that. The queen clearly wasn't a fan of things not going according to her plans.

Amber and Lily scrambled to their feet, and the wolves backed off barely enough to let them pass, growling lightly.

"We're not leaving you," Lily told me. She clutched me in a hug, and I awkwardly held the dagger out of the way. It probably didn't do much for my threatening stance.

"You can't do anything here," I whispered into her ear, refusing to say goodbye. I needed to believe I would get a chance to see her again. "Go get help."

I didn't really think the local police would be able to take on Moriath, but I needed to convince my sisters to get to safety.

"Okay." Lily squeezed me again and glanced back fearfully at the Unseelie Queen before grabbing Amber's hand and heading back up the tunnel.

"You better not die," muttered Amber as she was dragged past me. "You've got some explaining to do!"

I didn't answer her. I just kept my eyes and dagger trained on Moriath, desperately wishing it still contained power. Although, even if it had, one little blade in my untrained hands was pretty useless against that silver axe the dark warrior was casually resting on his shoulder.

"Bel," said the queen reasonably. "I'm not surprised that you've grown attached to the boy. He's always been a handsome lad, although it's a pity you couldn't have seen him before."

"Before your wolves almost killed him, you mean? Before you slaughtered his sister and tried to take his home from him?" I knew hate wasn't generally a constructive emotion, but, oh, did I hate her. I hated the pain she had brought to the people I loved, and I hated the familiar way she talked about Leith, as though she actually cared about him.

"Before he broke his vow to me, Bel."

Oh right, I also hated how she used my nickname like she was an old family friend, not someone who had manipulated my father into selling his children to her.

The queen continued mildly, "I know you humans break promises on a daily basis, but to the fae, a vow is a stronger magic than you can imagine. You can't break one without certain consequences."

"You tricked him into pledging himself to you," I hissed, my control slipping.

"Is that what he told you?" She tilted her head. "I'd be wary of investing too much emotion into such a change-able boy. Better that you forget him. Go find a nice human mate. Leith will join my wolves, and all will be as it should be." She tapped a finger lightly against her bottom lip.

"Maybe I'll keep him as a bear, but I don't know. They don't work as well with a pack. Well, I'll figure it out. Step aside, Bel."

I took a deep breath. "No."

"Pardon me?" Moriath looked genuinely baffled.

"No, you can't have him," I told her evenly. Why wasn't Leith making any protest of his own? I couldn't risk taking my eyes off the queen to look behind me. Surely, he hadn't given up now?

"Now, Bel," she started, in the tone I might use with the kids from reading club if they got a little too rowdy.

"Please stop calling me that. We aren't friends."

"You're not terribly polite, even for a human. And you're also not listening. Leith made a vow. He's mine."

I closed my eyes, remembering the way Leith had kissed me. Was it only hours ago? I thought of our winter afternoons spent reading, of the rare smiles that I managed to startle out of him. Some things were simply true, and I knew my next words were, without any chance of argument, truth.

"He isn't," I told her firmly, putting all my intention into my next words. "Leith is mine."

And with my words, I heard a crack, like the sound ice makes on a lake when it breaks apart. It echoed around the chamber and bounced back like a thousand small splinters of sound.

Moriath's eyes widened, and the flash of fire I'd seen earlier was back in them. She gave a snap of her fingers, and her wolves closed in around us. As the queen took a step forward, the low-level hum of magic that surrounded her intensified until it became painful.

The Unseelie Queen raised a hand, and all her jewels flashed. The weight of her power became too much to bear, and my dagger dropped from my useless fingers with a clatter.

I fell to my knees. What had I been thinking, trying to take on the Queen of the Unseelie Fae? I was just a girl, and very soon I'd be just a dead girl.

Suddenly the crushing magic lifted. As I gasped for breath, I was surprised to see Kylian whispering something into the queen's ear.

Moriath laughed. Not like an evil queen laugh, but a laugh of honest happiness, and somehow that was even more terrifying.

"It would seem you're right, Bel," she said, wiping a tear from the corner of her eye. "Leith is yours. I hope you enjoy your last moments together."

Chapter 34

I WHIRLED IN A PANIC TO SEE Leith behind me. My prince was back in his fae form. I'd broken the curse. But his injuries remained, and they were even worse than I had feared.

I fell down on my knees beside his unconscious body, and his blood soaked through the edges of my ruined dress.

Frantically, I felt for his pulse, leaning my cheek over his mouth to feel the faint stirring of his breath. I hadn't lost him yet, but his condition was far beyond my limited first aid skills. He needed help and quickly.

The hairs on the back of my neck stood on end, and I looked up from my panic to see Moriath leaning over us, eyeing both my wounded prince and me with interest.

"The Sapphires of Airmid," she began conversationally, fingering Neala's necklace. "I don't suppose Leith ever told you their history."

"Really?!" The word burst out of me in anger. "History? Don't you have better things to do than annoy me right now? Kingdoms to rule? Other lives to ruin?"

"I am very busy. It's true," the queen said with a laugh, "but I'm feeling generous today. The necklace's history actually applies to your current difficulties."

I glared at her, but she ignored it. "Airmid was one of the Danu, the first of the Tuatha Dé Danann. She was a powerful faerie and the champion of healers. This necklace was a creation of hers. It can heal any wound, no matter how mortal."

I stilled as her words set in. I had traded the very object that could have healed Leith as he lay bleeding behind me.

"It's a pity you don't have it anymore." The queen leaned down to smooth Leith's hair back from his forehead. I barely resisted the urge to slap her hand away. "But, as I said, I'm feeling generous. I'd be happy to save Leith." The queen paused thoughtfully. "In return for him coming back with me."

Of course, the only way she wanted Leith to live was in her possession. I put my hand on Leith's chest. His breaths seemed shallower than a minute ago. He had once told me he'd rather die than join Moriath's wolves.

But I was the one who would have to make the choice. Could I watch him die when there was any other option?

"What will you choose, Bel?" The queen looked down at me. "Do you love him enough to release him to me, if it will save his life?"

I did. I didn't know if Leith would forgive me, but I couldn't just let him die here in this cave. I tangled my fingers in his and whispered, "I'm sorry."

"What was that?" Moriath asked. "Have you made your choice?"

I had braced myself to say yes when I caught sight of Kylian behind the queen, the wolves arranged around him, watching us with interest. But it was the warrior who caught my attention. He widened his eyes at me and shook his head meaningfully.

What?

You can save him, the warrior mouthed at me.

I quickly dropped my eyes before the queen could notice our silent exchange. What did Kylian mean? I could still save Leith without the queen's bargain? How could I trust him?

And yet…how could I not try?

I felt a sense of peace as I faced the Queen.

"No."

"What?" she breathed, the word infused with ice.

"No," I repeated. "You can't have him."

Moriath locked her gaze on mine, and for a moment I thought she might drag Leith through the faerie gate anyway.

"Come, my queen," rumbled Kylian, swinging his silver axe up onto his shoulder. "Let him die in the arms of his love. A tragic end to be sure, but you know he'll be more trouble than he's worth if he's not bound to you."

Moriath rose stiffly, her narrowed eyes still fixed on Leith. She hesitated and then swept back toward the faerie gate.

"I suppose you're right. Fiachra won't be happy, but he'll have to be content with the boy being dead. Though it seems a waste." She ran her hand along the back of one of her wolves, who panted happily. Just before she stepped through the gate, she turned back to me one last time. "I hope you don't regret your choice, Bel. Kylian, seal the gate behind us."

With that she was gone. Her wolves bounded happily after her. Darkness swallowed us as she left, the cave lit only by the dim blue glow of Amber's phone, still lying in a corner.

Moriath's dark warrior hesitated in front of the gate.

"Help us!" I pleaded. I didn't know why he cared what happened to Leith, but he had seemed to be on my side earlier.

"I cannot," he said regretfully, turning to face me. "Moriath will already be noticing my delay in returning. But you can save him still. If you have the will."

"But there's no magic here." No magic. No hope.

"There is enough." And then he too stepped through the gate, leaving me and Leith alone in the dark cave.

My prince was lying in terrifying stillness. Even his chest was still now, no breath coming out of his mouth.

"No no no no no..." I pleaded. I fumbled at his neck, searching for a pulse. Finally, I stilled my frantic breathing enough to make out a faint heartbeat. He was still with me, if barely.

I lay down beside Leith in the dirt, my head on his chest, my eyes closed. I could still faintly hear his heart beating. Kylian had said I had enough magic to save him, but what did that mean? If only I had a way to get him to Faerie.

Leith's heartbeat grew slower. "Please don't take him from me now," I whispered into the dark. It seemed more than unfair that the world could contain magic and wonder and still have this much heartbreak in it.

And then, lying there in the stillness, I slowly sensed a soft buzzing behind me. The gate was powered on this side by the magic-infused gold plate. Could I use it to heal him? I focused my will on Leith's injuries and drew on the magic around me.

"Be healed," I pleaded with both the magic and the fae prince. Nothing. It wasn't enough. But I had more.

Shrugging my bag off, I dumped the contents out on the ground. The rose. Where was my rose? I found it as much by magic as touch, and the thorns impaled my palm as I grasped it tightly. It left a scattering of petals on the ground when I picked it up. The magic of Kilinaire must be fading.

"Please let this still hold enough magic!" I prayed. "And let my friends at Kilinaire still be safe. We're going to try this once more," I told Leith firmly, blinking back my tears. "And you're going to help me this time, okay? Okay."

I could feel him slipping away from me, but I put the rose on his chest, with my hand over it, and leaned over until my nose brushed against his.

"Be healed," I breathed. Then I closed my eyes and felt all the magic from the rose and the gate pull into me. I pressed my lips against his and let the magic pour into him, picturing him whole and healthy. The magic continued to run through me as I felt the rose crumble to dust in my hand, and the cave began to rumble as the faerie gate collapsed in on itself. It still wasn't enough. I pulled from the last bit of magic I could feel, from that spark deep within myself.

The rumbling turned to crashing as the cavern started to fall apart around us, the tunnel losing stability as the gate collapsed. But I barely noticed. I'd given everything I had, and as I slipped into unconsciousness, I felt the slightest movement of air against my lips.

Leith was breathing.

And then everything faded into the rising darkness.

CHAPTER 35

MY SISTERS SAVED US, I LEARNED LATER. They only got to the surface before starting to argue about whether they should run for help—Lily—or scour around for weapons and head back in—Amber. They were halfway back to us with a rusty pickaxe and an ancient shovel when they heard the tunnel caving in.

Lily told me that it was a surprise for them to find a one-eyed fae prince instead of a grizzly bear, but on the whole, preferable. Leith had regained enough strength to stumble out with Amber's help, but Lily had to carry me out.

My sisters wanted to take me to the hospital, but Leith convinced them I would be better off at Kilinaire and led them down the mountain and back through the Rose Gate.

I woke, as I have so often in my life, to Amber trying to be quiet. She's not very good at it.

"Should we wake him up?" my sister whispered loudly. Honestly, there are probably jet engines quieter than Amber whispering.

"We shall do no such thing, child," murmured Ena softly. "He hasn't slept in two days. Clear the plates from the table, and we'll leave them in peace."

"I just thought he'd want to know."

"Want to know what? Please try to avoid crashing the dishes together like that."

"That Bel's awake."

There was a meaningful pause.

"You're awake, right, Bel?" Amber hissed.

I cracked an eye reluctantly to find myself back in my old room at Kilinaire, the warm weight of Rani pressed up against my legs. I'd been asleep two days? It felt like about twenty minutes. I was still exhausted.

"See!" Amber gave a yelp as she was smacked on the leg by a small person beside her.

The stranger wore a simple green dress with a white apron and a white kerchief on her head. Her skin was mottled in shades of brown, and her long ears came to sharp points at the tops. Her dark eyes glittered merrily as she watched me sit up in the bed. All in all, she was no taller than...a raccoon.

"Ena?" I blinked in disbelief.

"Of course, my dear," the brownie answered briskly. "But do keep your voice down, if you please. As I told your impertinent younger sister, the prince badly needs his rest." She gestured behind her to where Leith was sprawled on the armchair by the fireplace, legs dangling over the chair's arm.

I drank in the sight of him, safe and whole. His dark hair was adorably messy, and his patch had slid off as he slept, leaving both of his closed eyelids exposed, one covered with scars, but both with dark smudges under them. Ena was right. He needed his sleep.

"Are you ready to get up, Bel?" whispered Amber, loudly. "Lily is making pancakes in this really short kitchen downstairs with a couple of...actually I have no idea what they are. They're blue, though, so that's pretty cool. This place is awesome. I can't believe you've been keeping it to yourself! Now, if I found a magic portal—"

"Or do you need to sleep still, my dear?" interrupted Ena, with a pointed look at Amber.

"Sorry! I'll be quieter. I'll just get this teacup, and I'll leave so quietly that..."

"She's always been like this," I whispered to Ena, apologetically. "You should have seen her as a kid. It was such a relief when she turned into a surly teenager and started sleeping in."

Amber finished clearing the side table and tiptoed toward the door. "You need to do something about your hair," she said as she passed me. "It's even rattier than normal."

Sweet, sweet Amber.

"Shall I leave you to sleep, then? Or would you like a day dress?" asked the brownie. "You used up most of your life's energy healing our prince. The magic of Faerie should have you nearly set to rights by now, but it does take some rest."

"As much as I would love more sleep, I have to use the bathroom." I swung my legs over the side of the bed, causing Rani to make a noise of protest and leap off the bed in search of a more peaceful place to nap. My stomach growled loudly. "And apparently I'd like those pancakes as well."

I found Lily and the pancakes in the kitchen with the formerly-beaver chefs, who were, in fact, blue. Lily crushed me with a hug and demanded I never scare her like that again, before feeding me apple pancakes drizzled with honey until I thought I might burst.

Deirdre met me down there to fix my hair. She proved to be a slim, green, waist-high faerie with leaves growing through her long hair. The former fox tutted over the bird's nest I'd made of my hair. Her long, twig-like fingers plucked out hairpins and untangled curls matted with glitter and dirt. I needed a bath soon to wash out the rest of my once-fancy hairstyle, but I was impatient to see the rest of the castle, free from its hundred-year curse. Deirdre settled for a braid, tied with a green ribbon and a whispered word of magic to keep it in place.

Once Lily was finished stuffing me with pancakes and scolding me for nearly dying back in the mine, she dragged me out the kitchen door to "talk where we can stand up straight." She continued lecturing me outside, but I barely heard her. All my attention was captured by the view in front of me.

The gardens and orchards were back where they belonged, with bees happily buzzing in the sunshine. On closer inspection, not all the small flying things were insects and birds. Little faeries with wings like those of butterflies and cicadas flitted around the garden. Were those the piskies Ena had told me about? Past the orchards, the aurochs grazed contentedly in the spring green pasture. Beyond the giant cattle, the pasture turned to forest, and in the distance, towering blue mountains rose out of the forest, tall enough to be capped with snow, even in this late spring heat.

Lily trailed off.

"Bel?" She put her hand on my arm. "Are you alright? You're crying."

I nodded, tears streaming down my cheeks. "I'm fine. I'm great. I just didn't know there were mountains."

I gave Lily a tour of the grounds even though she had obviously grown comfortable at Kilinaire during my two-day nap. Everything was familiar, but at the same time, so changed. Pastures and copses of trees surrounded the castle grounds on all sides, and faeries, ranging from small to tiny, scurried about putting the grounds to rights. A tall brown faerie who reminded me of an oak tree was ordering around packs of little flying faeries in the rose garden. He must be Geanan. Leaves flew as the hedges were trimmed into strict order.

I pulled Lily along the gravel path. I wanted to show her the fountain with the statue of the winged lady. When we arrived in the middle of the hedge maze, Amber was there conversing with a small brown otter.

"Tait!" I ran up and gave the little otter a hug before letting him squirm back down to the ground. "Wait, why are you still an otter? What happened?"

"Oh, Isobel." Tait hung his head mournfully. "I think something went wrong! Everyone else is a faerie again, and I'm still…furry."

"Oh no. Maybe we can bring Clíodhna to check you out." I fussed over him, trying to think of what could have caused him to be still affected by the curse. "Do you think…"

Tait was still looking at me with sad puppy eyes, but Amber was trying very hard to avoid eye contact with me.

"Wait a minute…"

Amber slapped her hand over her mouth to hold in her laughter. And I smacked Tait across the top of his head.

"You're just fine, aren't you, phouka?"

Amber's giggles burst out of her as the little otter changed briefly into a long-tailed black creature that looked like a cross between a large cat and a shaggy bunny, before shifting into a colorful bird and leaping into the sky to avoid another smack from me.

"It was her idea!" yelled the bird.

"Traitor!" Amber shook her fist at the bird's retreating form.

"It never stops with that one."

I turned at the voice I loved best in the world to see Leith coming up behind us through the hedges.

"I apologize, but I must steal your sister," he said to Amber and Lily. "We have much to discuss."

CHAPTER 36

I MUST ADMIT, I WAS A BIT nervous about what Leith would want to discuss. So much had happened since his disaster of a birthday party, but had he forgiven me?

He twined his long fingers through mine as we walked through the garden, which made my heart beat faster. All right then, he didn't hate me.

After we walked a reasonable distance from my sisters, at the walled edge of the garden, I spun around to look at my prince.

"Bear, I'm so sorr—"

My apology was abruptly cut off as Leith bent down and kissed me. Not still angry, then. I wrapped my arms around his neck as he pressed me back against the cool stone garden wall.

"Thank you," he whispered, kissing the corner of my mouth. "Thank you for not giving up on me. You saved me, Isobel. You saved all the faeries of Kilinaire, and for that I'll never be able to repay you."

"You're not still upset about your birthday?" My brain was scrambling to catch up. "I didn't mean to hurt you. I'm sorry I made our first kiss so weird."

"I'm the one who's sorry." Leith leaned his forehead against mine. "After Moriath manipulated me so badly, I couldn't bear the thought of someone else playing games with me. I'd loved you since I saw you in the forest that day, surrounded by those wolves. That you might have only seen me as a puzzle to solve..." He closed his eye. "That's no excuse though. Please forgive my wounded pride and terrible behavior."

"You love me?"

"I do," he responded solemnly.

"I love you, too." I pressed a kiss against his fingers, suddenly shy.

"I thought I heard something to that effect. Back in the mine, shortly before I all but died," Leith teased.

"Not my favorite night." I shivered, remembering his heartbeat fading away under my hand.

"It wasn't all bad." He smirked. "I also remember you telling Moriath I was yours now."

I blushed, still looking at our entwined fingers. "Well, aren't you?"

He tipped my chin up and looked me steadily in the eyes. "Now and forever," he answered, all joking gone from his tone. And then he kissed me deeply once more in a way that erased all my doubts.

We stayed at Kilinaire another few days, letting the magic of Faerie replenish what I had given of myself back in the mine. I slept late into the mornings and took an embarrassing number of afternoon naps, until I felt more like myself again and Ena pronounced me well enough to go home.

Amber made gagging noises as I said goodbye to Leith, promising to be back as soon as I could. He reminded me between kisses that every moment I was gone would literally be hours for him. My sisters eventually lost their patience and dragged me through the Rose Gate.

Amber was making us laugh with a story about Tait as we tromped through the woods. The two of them got into enough trouble separately. The thought of them as friends was a bit terrifying. But when we reached the edge of our back yard, we sobered up quickly. We stood in the waist-high ferns, golden in the August heat, and regarded our little house.

It was just how I'd left it. The window was still smashed, the door still hanging crookedly on broken hinges.

I shivered, thinking of the Unseelie Queen's henchmen crashing through my home.

We stood there in somber silence, and then Lily put an arm around each of our waists and hugged us to her.

"Now, ladies. It doesn't look good. I'll give you that. But things aren't so dismal. We might not have parents who are worthy of us. We might not have a house that feels safe. But that doesn't mean we aren't a family, and it doesn't mean we don't have a home. We have each other." She gave us a squeeze. "We'll visit Dad in the hospital and tell him we're fine on our own. Amber, Bel and I are old enough to get legal custody of you. Right, Bel?"

I nodded, blinking back tears. I might be able to forgive our father, in time, but that didn't mean I wanted him raising Amber. It was time for me to start paying more attention to my little sister, before I lost her down the dark path I was seeing more and more glimpses of.

"Right," I told them both firmly.

"We'll fix up the cabin again." Lily headed toward the house, the two of us in tow. "I always hated that door anyway. We should paint the new one blue. But first I'll bake some cookies. Us Watson girls have each other. And we'll be all right. Okay?"

"Okay." I squeezed her hand.

"They'd better be snickerdoodles," groused Amber, rubbing tears out of her eyes.

"Is there any other kind?" teased Lily, and together we went home, to make something better out of the pieces of our former life.

One sunny afternoon, Kilinaire time, Leith and I hauled our books—*Vampire Academy* for me, *Modern Bee-keeping* for him—and a picnic tea up to the top of the back tower.

All my intentions for reading were lost, however, as soon as I got to the top of the tower and was transfixed by the view. At my back were the wild forests and mountains that separated the Rose Court from the Unseelie kingdom. It seemed foolish to assume the icy queen had given up on her schemes, even if she no longer had any right to Leith or my sisters and me.

But I didn't have it in me to be consumed with worries, not on a day like today. I leaned on the stone wall of the tower and looked out over the rolling farmlands to the south, dotted with trees and cut through with the shining blue of the river. Over the bridge, a dirt road led to the village. Leith had promised to take me in a few days when he visited next. He was busy these days, catching up on how the farmers and villagers had fared while he was trapped in the castle. The Seelie King had installed one of his men to manage the area, and while King Fiachra claimed to be happy that the curse had been lifted, Leith suspected the king was reluctant to hand Leith's lands back to him. I told Leith about Moriath's comment about the Seelie King, but neither of us knew what she meant by it. Questions for another day.

The prince came up beside me, glancing out at the view before leaning back against the wall to study me.

"You're awfully serious, Bear." I laughed. "What is it?"

"Isobel," he began solemnly.

"Leith," I teased, trying to school my expression into one matching his seriousness and failing.

"Marry me."

"What?" I squeaked.

"Marry me," he repeated. "You said it before. We belong to each other. Stay in Kilinaire."

I struggled to form a coherent sentence. "But...I'm only eighteen! Were you ready to get married at eighteen? How long ago was that? Jeepers, there's a bit of an age gap here, isn't there?"

"I wasn't ready to get married at eighteen, no," he admitted. "Because I hadn't met you yet. And yes, I'm more than a hundred years older than you. It doesn't matter. Stay in Faerie and live to be a thousand." He brushed his lips against my ear, causing me to shiver, and whispered, "Think how many books you could read."

I laughed in spite of myself. "An excellent point."

"But you're not saying yes." He turned back to the view.

"I'm not saying no, either," I countered.

He looked back at me, hope written across his face. "But?" he prompted.

"I need to stay with Lily and Amber for now. I've already enrolled for online college courses, so I can stay in Pilot Bay until Amber graduates high school." I leaned against his shoulder. "And then I have two more years at University to finish my degree and become a librarian."

"This is sounding like a very long time," he muttered. "How long until Amber finishes her schooling?"

"Two years."

"Two years then," he said firmly. "And then you'll come live at Kilinaire."

I opened my mouth to speak.

He pressed a finger to my lips. "Two years, which I must remind you will feel like an eternity in faerie time, and once we're married, you can go to school anywhere you want. Or have you forgotten that I have a magic portal?"

Because, of course, the Rose Gate wasn't only linked to my own faerie gate in the forest anymore. I wondered where all the other gates were, in Tír na nÓg and in the human world. I could suddenly see my future spreading out in front of me, and it was a good one.

School, travel, visits with my sisters, that giant magical library two stories below us in the tower, and most of all, Leith. I wanted that.

"Yes," I whispered, feeling like my heart might burst with happiness.

"Yes?" Leith repeated, a look of incredulous joy on his face.

I wound my arms around my prince's neck and pressed my lips to his in answer. Enough with the talking, it was time to get to the happily ever after.

HANNA SANDVIG

EPILOGUE

CLÍODHNA CONTENTEDLY SIPPED HER TEA AT HER favorite table at Pie in the Sky. The one by the window, with the best view of the people passing by. Like that sweet Isobel Watson and Clío's handsome godson on their way over to enjoy some pie with her. So good to see him out and about after all those years trapped at Kilinaire.

A bit awkward in jeans and a T-shirt perhaps, but he looked willing to put up with just about anything for his true love—and if that charming Chris Hemsworth could pull off an eye patch, then surely that made it a stylish enough accessory for a prince.

Truly, Isobel and Leith were even cuter together in person than when she had first glimpsed them in her mirror and begun her matchmaking. A nice bit of work, that. A solid blow to Moriath and a happy ending for one of her godchildren. She'd enjoy her well-earned apple pie and get back to work. After all, she had two faerie kingdoms to put to rights, and Tiernan didn't seem to be saving himself.

He'd need a little nudge. They always did.

Author's Note

YOU MADE IT TO THE END! I'm hoping that means that you enjoyed The Rose Gate. If you did, please leave a review. Reviews will help other readers to find this book. Apart from a purchase, it's the biggest way you can help out your favourite authors.

My version of Tír na nÓg is loosely based on Irish folklore. If you'd like to learn more about the world and the faeries that inhabit it, go to my website where you can find a map and a list of the various races with a little bit about each of them.

At my website you can also see illustrations I drew for the paperback edition, and sign up for my newsletter. I use my newsletter it to send you updates on my books, peeks at upcoming art, and fun printables.

www.HannaSandvig.com

Thank you Sonya for this gorgeous comic page!
You can find out more about her comic, Druin Saga,
on Instagram at **@Sonya_Lindsay_Art**

A CHRISTMAS ENGAGEMENT

ARE YOU READY?" I PAUSED, MY HAND ON the doorknob of the back door. Our little house was glowing from within, twinkle lights lining every window and door, with candles on all the windowsills.

"Do I need to be ready?" asked Leith. "Isn't it just your sisters?"

"Well, yes. It's just...it's your first Christmas. I want it to be perfect."

"*Àlainn.*" He was dressed in his "human" clothes, dark jeans and a black coat. No glamour though, because we weren't going out, so his ears were still pointed. Snow was building up on his shaggy, dark hair. "Can we please go inside now. It looks much warmer in there."

"Okay." I took a deep breath. "Let's go."

I opened the door, and pulled Leith into the warmth of the cabin. The air smelled like gingerbread, and the husky voice of Ella Fitzgerald singing *White Christmas* drifted from the kitchen. Lily and Amber had still been asleep when I snuck out to Kilinaire to fetch Leith this morning, but Lily must be up and baking. Again.

It was our first Christmas with just us sisters. Mom

had sent us a postcard from Barbados, and we hadn't heard from Dad since he had said goodbye after checking out from the hospital.

Lily told us repeatedly that she was fine, but she couldn't seem to stop baking all the same. As if she could give us the perfect Christmas by making enough shortbread. She would laugh and say it was cheaper than therapy, but I was still keeping an eye on her.

"Merry Christmas!" Lily beamed at us as we entered the kitchen, our snowy boots and jackets left in the entryway. She was pouring a generous glug of eggnog into a snowman mug.

Amber sat at the table, eyes mostly closed, wrapped in a quilted satin blanket she had pilfered from Kilinaire. Another good reason for the constant baking was that it helped heat our little house. It had once been our summer cottage and was only heated by the fireplace in the living room and space heater upstairs. And, currently, gingerbread. Amber mumbled something incoherent and Lily slid the mug toward her.

"Christmas coffee?" she asked Leith, pouring another cup of vile brown liquid.

"I'm not sure what that is?" Leith had been introduced to coffee, but not *Christmas* coffee.

"It's not safe, don't trust it." I brushed past Amber, patting her messy bed-head on the way, and filled the kettle from the sink.

"Psssh, live a little." Lily plopped a Santa mug in

Leith's hand.

He studied the mug for a minute, then took a hesitant sip.

"It's delicious!" he said in surprise, with a smile for Lily.

"Noo, don't join the dark side!" But I couldn't stop grinning. I loved this. While visiting Kilinaire never stopped being amazing, there was something so perfect about seeing my prince here, with my family.

"Time for presents!" sang Lily.

"Mmm?" Amber perked up hopefully from her blanket nest.

I poured boiling water into a reindeer mug and bobbed the tea bag on its string a couple times.

"Isn't it too early?" I teased them both.

Lily gave me a dark look.

"She's been waiting impatiently all month," I told Leith. "Lily's the worst at keeping secrets. I think she's told everyone what everyone else is getting at least three times."

"I know." Leith took another sip of coffeenog. "She told me what she got you last week."

"Oooh, what is it?"

"Find out for yourself," Lily scolded, herding us out of the kitchen. "To the living room!"

The living room was, like the rest of the house, a very mismatched but festive room. Our couch hailed from the eighties, which fit in perfectly with the thrifted ornaments and multicolored strings of lights that Lily swore were "retro." But our tree was so beautiful that some might say it looked magical. And they would be correct because it was actually from Faerie. I had found it while out on a hike with Leith near Kilinaire Castle and had begged him to help me haul it back through the Rose Gate. The tree sparkled with little sheerie lights, twinkling and dancing softly around the flocked reindeer and satin balls on the branches.

Lily had found me a vintage copy of Dracula, with the most beautiful cloth bound cover and yellowed pages. Amber gave me a curling iron and a scrap of paper with a list of YouTube videos to teach me to use said curling iron.

"Because, honestly, Bel. Your hair."

I just gave her a kiss and a thank you. I knew she loved me, even if she was too prickly to admit it more than once or twice a decade. While my sisters opened their gifts from each other, I dug Leith's present out from under the tree.

"For you!" I plopped the snowman covered package on Leith's lap and settled beside him on the couch.

"Just a minute." Leith reached into his pocket and pulled out a round object which he placed in my hand.

"Is this a walnut?" The little nut was polished smooth and tied together with a strip of silk ribbon.

"Open it."

"You open yours first."

"I really think—"

"Oh my goodness! Just open them together!" Amber paused in her paper ripping to hiss at us.

Leith grimaced in mock terror at me, and we both started to tug the ribbons off our gifts.

I carefully opened the walnut to find a gold ring on a tiny cushion of moss.

I opened my mouth in a soundless "Oh", and picked up the ring. It was shining gold in an intricate knotwork pattern. I held it up to the light, wondering if it was magical.

I looked up at Leith in happiness to find him holding up his present with a puzzled expression.

"I, um, may have misjudged the price point for this gift exchange," I said with an embarrassed laugh.

He gave me a quizzical look.

"It's a Christmas sweater!"

He raised his eyebrow.

"They are, um, a traditional human Christmas... tradition."

"I can't believe you found one all in black." Amber leaned forward, still wrapped in her stolen blanket. "Well, except for the Santa hats."

"I know! And look, it has bears!" I pointed to the polar bears marching across the sweater front.

"Do you have a traditional human Christmas sweater?" asked Leith.

"I have three, actually."

"And yet, you're wearing a red dress."

"With polka dots. It's very festive."

"Yes, Bel, why aren't you wearing the sweater I made you last year?" asked Lily.

I stifled a shudder. Ah yes, the year Lily took up knitting. So tragic it didn't stick.

"I'll wear it later?"

"Maybe not until after we visit Kilinaire," Amber said, her eyes wide with remembered horror.

"Do you like the ring?" Leith murmured in my ear, causing me to shiver.

"It's the most beautiful thing I've ever owned," I answered softly, holding it up to the light.

"Your sisters told me that it's a human custom for a ring to symbolize a promise of marriage. You *do* still want to marry me, I hope?"

"Of course!" I had never been so sure of anything in my life.

"Good." Leith took the ring from me and slid it onto my finger. He leaned forward and brushed his lips over mine lightly. I wrapped my arms around his neck and pulled him down for a proper kiss. His lips were warm and I found that I liked the taste of eggnog and coffee after all.

"Come on, Bel!" Amber grabbed my arm and tugged me up the path toward the Rose Gate. The forest was a winter wonderland. The sun had come out, twinkling on the knee-deep drifts of snow between the trees. The aspen trees were bare and pale, and the conifers were blanketed in fresh snow.

We followed in the tracks of Lily and Leith, who had left after breakfast. Lily had muttered something about helping with dinner, but I wasn't sure what she was up to. It was only the end of autumn in Tír na nÓg, no special holiday.

"Why are you in such a hurry?" I pulled back against Amber's tugging.

"Why are you so nosy?" she retorted. "And slooooow."

We reached the Rose Gate, the enchanted roses still blooming despite their snowy dusting.

"Wait!" Amber pulled me back before I could walk through.

"I thought you were in some kind of rush?" I said, annoyed.

Amber held up a hand to shush me and leaned closer to a velvety red rose, watching carefully as the bloom slowly unfurled. And then watched some more.

"Okay, now!" She grabbed my arm again and pulled me through. I pushed my curiosity aside and thought fiercely of Kilinaire and its pale stone towers and hedge maze. Now that the curse had been lifted, the fairy gate wasn't only linked to Kilinaire. When a gate could lead anywhere, you had to concentrate to be sure that you

327

ended up in the right place.

We stepped out of winter and into late autumn, the trees at Kilinaire bare and the roses wilted except the ones that twined around the stone arch above us.

But Kilinaire castle was still beautiful, and I could see the cozy glow from the diamond-paned windows as we walked down the gravel path.

"Bel!" A chipmunk leapt from a tree, transforming mid jump into a little otter to bound along beside us. "Wait till you see—"

"Not a peep out of you, Tait!" Amber fixed the phouka with a fierce glare.

"But she's going to find out in a minute anyway," my little friend said mournfully.

"In the castle!" Amber ordered.

"Fine, fine. I never get to do anything..." Tait's grumbling trailed off as he transformed into a cardinal and flew ahead of us to the castle.

"Aren't we just coming for dinner?" I gave Amber my best big sister glare but she was, as always, immune.

"Well. There *is* a dinner." Amber pushed open one of the wooden doors and hauled me inside.

I gasped. The front foyer was covered in greenery and little twinkling *sheerie* lights. Dark green boughs spilled down the sides of the stairs with glowing lanterns on each step and garlands topping the doorways.

"Upstairs!" ordered Amber, pulling me past the doorway to the parlor.

"Is that Prince Tiernan?" I caught a glimpse of red hair and the prince gave me a mischievous smile before I was hauled away. I had met Leith's best friend a handful of times since the curse had been broken, but it was a surprise to see him here today.

"Later. We need to get you ready."

"Ready for what?" I followed her up the stairs and down the hallway to the Blue Room where I still stayed whenever I visited Kilinaire.

Deidre was waiting inside for me, with all her ribbons and sparkly hair clips ready. It had taken a while to adjust to her transformation from a fox to a slender willow tree sprite—a Sidhe Draoi—but in either form, no one could do hair like Deidre.

"I'll do her makeup, you work on her hair," Amber told the ladies maid, who nodded and got to work.

"Are *you* going to tell me what's going on?" I asked Deirdre as she ran her twig-like fingers through my hair, magically easing out the tangles and leaving it in silky waves.

"I am under strict orders from Lord Leith," she told me in her soft, thickly-accented voice.

"Hmmm."

"Turn." Amber started applying makeup while Deirdre wove dark red roses and sprigs of greenery into my hair, braiding the whole thing into a crown with little star spangled pins sprinkled throughout.

"Um, I'm not getting married today…right?" There

was an edge of panic in my voice. I had meant it when I told Leith that I wanted to marry him this morning. But I had also meant it earlier when I told him that I wanted to wait until Amber was done with high school. I couldn't leave her when she was still hurting so badly from losing our mom. She needed family, and Lily shouldn't have to raise her alone.

Amber just laughed. "Trust me, Bel, when you get married, I will have a much bigger makeup kit along."

"Then what—"

"Here's the dress!" Ena burst into the Blue Room through the lower half of the door built for shorter faeries. The brownie was carrying an armload of gauzy red fabric with dark brown leather boots stacked on top.

"Perfect timing." Amber dusted my face with something powdery. "She's ready to go."

"Go where?" I wailed, not actually expecting a response by this point.

"Come try the dress on," said Ena, setting the boots down by the doorway.

I slipped out of my jersey Christmas dress and Deirdre helped me into the gown. The bodice was dark red velvet with knotwork in gold edging the neckline and fitted velvet sleeves. The skirt belled out in layers of lighter red gauzy silk with golden stars scattered on it to match the ones in my hair.

"Ena. This is the most beautiful dress I've ever worn." I knelt to give the brownie a hug.

"It did turn out rather well," agreed Ena briskly. "Now for the boots and coat."

The boots were clearly leipreachán made and the buttery leather fit perfectly. The coat was dark red wool, almost like a dress itself with a full skirt and fur trimmed hood and sleeves. It was very cozy.

"So we're going outside?" I asked hopefully, my cheeks flushing from the warmth of the fireplace and all my layers.

"You girls are," confirmed Ena. "Deirdre and I need to put the finishing touches on dinner."

Amber pulled on her gray peacoat and grabbed my arm again.

"Thank you!" I called to my faerie friends as I was hauled out of the room.

"Have you seen Tait anywhere?" I faintly heard Ena ask Deirdre behind us. "Trust that one to be scarce when there's work to be done."

When we passed the parlor again, it was empty except for a couple of piskies flitting about and stealing candy from a side table.

Amber led me back outside to the Rose Gate.

"Don't I need to know where I'm going?" I asked.

"Just hold tight!" And with that, Amber plunged us both through the gate.

We emerged into a misty forest at the base of a grass-covered hill. The trees surrounding the hill were ancient and covered with moss and little mushrooms. At first glance, the forest was empty, but flashes of movement in the corners of my eyes told me that some of the *Aos Sí*—the small folk—were nearby. The sun was near the treetops, visible between the drifting misty clouds. Leith had taken me to a few places in Tír na nÓg since the curse had been broken, but I'd never been here before.

I turned to ask Amber where we were, only to find her halfway up the hill, and Leith at my side instead. He was, shockingly, wearing black. The jeans and button-up from this morning had been replaced by formal wear, with polished black leather boots and a cloak with dark gray fur across the shoulders. Here was the source of today's mysteries. I gave him a mock glare, but it was impossible to be annoyed when really, I loved surprises.

"Care to let me in on the secret?" I asked him frostily. He just grinned at me, warming me through. He smiled more these days, but I still treasured every one.

"Engagement rings are a human custom." He tucked my hand into the crook of his arm. "In Faerie, we do things differently."

We walked together up a path edged with stones to the top of the hill. A little red squirrel ran ahead of us, giving me a wink as he passed. I laughed. Of course Tait couldn't resist being in on the secret.

My sisters waited on the hilltop with Tiernan. The redheaded prince gave me a wink when he caught my eye. Flirt.

Between them was a lone standing stone, about as tall

as my chin. It was an ancient-looking thing, with strange swirling symbols carved into every inch of its surface.

"So this is how faeries get engaged?" I asked my prince when we reached the top of the hill. The standing stone had a hole in it, near the top. I crouched down and looked through. Leith went around to the other side and ducked down to peek at me with his good eye.

"Not exactly."

We both straightened and Leith offered me his scarred left hand through the hole.

I hesitantly grasped it with my own left hand and he gave a slight tug, pulling until our clasped hands were in the heart of the stone.

The runes covering the stone started to glow and I could feel the hum of magic in my bones radiating out from my hand.

"Um, what does this do, exactly?"

"Why?" Leith sounded amused. "Are you worried?"

I opened my mouth to say that of course I wasn't worried, that was ridiculous. I had fought wolves and faced the Unseelie Queen. What was a little glowing rock?

But what came out of my mouth was a soft "A little."

I gave the glowing stone a sharp look. "That's not what I meant to say."

"The magic of the standing stone makes it impossible to tell anything but the truth," Leith explained. "Try lying. What's your favorite color?"

I tried with all my might to say blue. "Yellow."

"It's the custom for the *Tuatha Dé Danann* to pledge themselves to each other through a *fáinne menhir*. This prevents unions built on treachery or greed. But it also creates the beginnings of a strong bond, that's completed during the wedding ceremony."

"So...I can ask you anything, and you'll have to answer truthfully?"

"That's right." The gleam in his gray eye matched the one in mine.

"Ask him what actually happened to my favorite slingshot when we were eleven!" piped up Tiernan.

"Ask her where my purple scarf is!" added Amber.

"Hush, both of you," whispered Lily.

"Bear." I looked him in the eye.

"*Àlainn,*" he responded in the same tone.

"When did you know that you loved me?"

"When you attacked Moriath's wolves with a pitchfork. I was stunned. You were such a little thing, with no reason to help me."

"That long ago?" I gasped.

Leith just nodded.

"Why didn't you say anything? Months, it took you! Months!"

"I had no reason to think that you felt anything for me but fear. And then..."

"Yes?"

"I didn't think I truly deserved to be happy. Not like this." He ran his thumb over my knuckles.

"Oh, Leith," I whispered.

"Are these things always this sappy?" Amber whispered loudly to Tiernan.

"This one is especially so," the prince responded.

Normally I'd make a face at my little sister, but I couldn't pull my gaze away from Leith's. I loved every inch of his face, from his silver gray eye to his full bottom lip. Even his scars, because I couldn't imagine him without the strength he had learned from them.

"I need to give you a haircut," I murmured.

"Okay, you don't need to say every true thing that comes to mind." Tiernan rolled his eyes. "Leith, do you swear that you are entering this engagement with pure intentions? That you love Isobel and desire to marry her for no reason but to bring her happiness?"

"I swear it is true," Leith said, watching me solemnly.

"And Isobel, do you swear that you are entering this engagement with pure intentions? That you love Leith and aren't just marrying him for his fancy castle and lovely collection of honey bees?"

"Is this the standard set of engagement questions?" I asked Tiernan. He just smiled back innocently.

"I do swear that." I looked back to Leith. "I'd marry you and live in a shack."

"We already do," muttered Amber.

I felt a warmth flare up around our joined hands and, with a shock, realized that I could feel Leith across from me, his emotions an echo of my own happiness.

"Kiss! kiss! kiss!" called Lily.

We let go of each other's hands, and the symbols on the stone slowly faded, but the connection I felt in my heart to Leith was still there, vibrating between us.

Leith pulled me around the stone and into his arms.

"I truly, truly love you." I looked up at him and he gave a little half smile, leaning his forehead against mine. I could feel his response without words.

I wrapped my arms around his neck and lifted my face for a kiss. As his lips met mine, I felt something cold on my forehead. I looked up to see the first snowfall of Tír na nÓg's winter drifting down around us, each snowflake twinkling in the golden glow of the setting sun.

Late that night, after a feast of roast goose at Kilinaire, Leith and I sat on the couch in my living room. We each had our books, and we were reading by the light of the faerie Christmas tree and the multicolored lights overhead. Rani had followed us home and the little gray cat lounged contentedly on the back of the couch.

We had changed out of our finery and Leith was wearing the sweater I had given him. He should have looked funny, but he just looked even more delicious with polar bears marching across his chest.

I looked less amazing with my knobbly green and red sweater from Lily pulled over my comfy red dress. I had only planned to wear it long enough to make her happy, but now that both my sisters were in bed, I had to admit that it was actually rather cozy.

"So, Bear." I gave up trying to read and closed my book in my lap.

He looked up at me expectantly.

"How was your first Christmas? Did it live up to your hopes and dreams?"

He set his book down as well and picked up my hand, running a thumb over the knotted golden ring.

"Well, the present from your sisters was especially touching."

Lily and Amber had bought him an ornament shaped like a teddy bear with the words "Baby's First Christmas" on its belly. They had personalized it by crossing out "baby" and writing "Leith" on it in sharpie. They had also given the bear an eyepatch.

"I hope we weren't too crazy for you," I said with a wince.

"Oh, just wait and see what I got you all for Solstice." His amusement hummed across our bond, and I snuggled up to my prince, sure that no one had ever had a Christmas as good as this one.

THE END

Acknowledgements

S O MANY THANK-YOUS! First off, thank you dear readers for taking a chance on a debut author's book. You're the reason I wrote this book, and I appreciate you more than I can say.

Thank you, Mom, for being such a great mentor to me during the whole publishing process. I don't know what I would have done without your advice and support. Everyone go find Valerie Comer on Amazon and read all her books, they're wonderful.

Thank you to my first readers! Craig, my amazing husband who always supports my creativity and told me that the manuscript was amazing as many times as I needed to hear it. Sonya, for taking long walks with me to talk about plot issues. Julie, for harassing me to write faster. Mar, for all your detailed notes and being an amazing accountability partner.

Thank you to my Beta Readers: Kari, Stephanie, Victoria, Paula, and Rachel, your feedback was invaluable!

Thank you to my editor, Nicole, for all your hard work trying to teach a newbie writer how to use commas, spell things like an American, and a million other things that have made this book infinitely better and more enjoyable to read.

Thank you to Carrie, Elizabeth, Christine, Rebecka, Genevieve, Lisa, Faith, Priscila, Rachel, Crystal, Rebecca, Emma, Sandra, Virginia, Sheala, and Zerin for helping me clean up this book for the second edition.

But most of all, thank you God, for creating a world that inspires, and giving me a creative spirit and stories to tell. I hope this one makes you smile.

About The Author

HANNA SANDVIG IS TURNING your favorite fairy tales into faerie tales with some sweet romance and enough sass to keep things interesting.

Hanna is living out her personal happily-ever-after in the mountains of BC, Canada with her husband, three little girls, and giant cat. When she's not writing, drawing, or reading, she can be found sewing, taking photos, baking, and desperately trying to not pick up any more creative pursuits.

If you drop in to visit, please bring plenty of chocolate and strong black tea.